Into the Magic Cornfield

A Heather Hazelkind Story

TODD BERNACIL

Into the Magic Cornfield: A Heather Hazelkind Story
Copyright © 2018 by Todd Eugene Bernacil

978-1-7339918-4-1 (paperback)
978-1-7339918-2-7 (ebook)

DEDICATION

I dedicate this book with love to all the children who read it, especially my little nephew, Sebastian Bernacil. Adults alike. When reading, know that there will always be someone somewhere who loves you, even in the darkest corners of life, and that you are never alone. Know that being special comes from the heart. I welcome you all into my magic land.

PART I
The Cornfield

CHAPTER

1

There lived a lovely young elementary school teacher named Ms. Heather Hazelkind who had shiny black hair and brassy brown eyes. She loved to take her students on countryside field trips every year, for Nebraska was the autumn heaven of Heather's childhood.

The cornfields would stretch out over the flatlands and billow like a green ocean. The largest maizefield came from Hagglehoff Farm. Everyone in the local area knew about its fine reputation of Holt County.

In May, before the start of the hot season, Heather took the young pupils on a bus trip to the Hagglehoff Farm on the outskirts of town.

They were delighted.

That bright sunny day, Heather was in a plain white blouse with a beige undershirt and a light brown skirt. She always carried with her a dark brown shoulder bag with necessities. Plainness didn't seem to bother her as she assumed natural beauty.

Everyone loved her kindness and stark sense of dignity. Her little students had great respect for her. She was very patient with them and made sure they weren't left behind in their studies, and also made sure they were mentally and physically healthy. She delicately counseled parents who had issues with their child. Most importantly, she made sure the children understood what it meant to be good people. During the beginning, middle, and end of the school year, she would always say to them, "Remember, class, everything you do in life means something, no matter how old you are. The things you do, whether good or bad, not only affect you but everyone around you. So, mind what you do and make the best of who you are wherever you go."

After passing a large weather vane, the bus pulled up to the Hagglehoff Farm.

The children filed out the vehicle and were greeted by the friendly farm manager who had a stout figure. "Good morning, little fellas." He had chubby cheeks and spoke jovially. "Welcome to the farm of my uncle, William Hagglehoff, the genius who created this huge land. I am his successor, Jake Patterson. I would be glad to guide you through this tour on such a bright day. Let's go, folks!"

The tour was enriching. Gem-like fruit tasted lastingly sweet. Cows yielded gallons of fresh, warm milk. In fact, Heather delighted in purchasing a jar of it to use in her recipes at home. The children playfully scurried about the plumb pumpkin patch. One pumpkin even weighed two tons!

At last, it was time to traverse the great cornfields in a farm wagon pulled by Mr. Jake Patterson in a tractor. The children packed into the wagon like sardines while Heather sat at the edge in the back, overlooking the glimmering stalks with razor-sharp leaves. The driver fired up the engine, which startled the hares nearby, and the party slowly rode along the rugged ground, leaving clouds of dust behind.

"Hope you're having fun, kids," Farmer Patterson said into the microphone attached to his earpiece. "We should be picking up speed in a little bit."

The wagon headed into the heart of the cornfields on a wide trail. Heather mused over the mysterious green field, as if it were speaking to her, when the farm cart hit a good-sized rock on the dusty road.

"Whoops! Sorry about that, folks," said Farmer Patterson over the speaker. The flimsy doorlatch directly behind her loosened and the iron-gate was set free, though no one noticed it open. The tractor picked up more speed.

"Look to your left, folks." Farmer Patterson pointed to a large flock of blackbirds soaring gracefully together in a sinuous pattern at a distance. The children were amused by the spectacle. The iron door quietly swung outward and inward with no one paying any attention to the back of the wagon. "Hang on tight, kids. Let's see if we could get a better look."

Farmer Patterson began to make a sharp left turn toward the flock and the children held onto the railing while watching the birds. By then, the iron-gate was wide open and Heather tried to lean against it during the turn, but instead tumbled out into the edge of the trail with no one noticing her fall.

As she got to her feet, Heather heard the wagon continue its course, but could not see it. The cornstalks surrounded her. She hollered after the wagon, but it didn't return. The tapering noise of her ride quickly became no more. She was all alone in the giant cornfield.

A glowering scarecrow she didn't remember seeing earlier towered above her with hollowed-out eyes. Its weathered face was callous, as if it were unhappy being stuck on a wooden pole all its life. The lackluster clothing tattered over time from the sun-ridden sky. The seeping corn stuffing resembled wriggly worms. Oddly enough, the dummy's face looked eerily human, even though Heather knew this to only be a clever trick to scare off the pestering crows. "My!" she thought to herself. "His face looks so real!"

She scurried down the paths of maize, but could not see any trail from the wagon. Panicked, Heather thought that she either lost her sense of direction, or the trail disappeared behind her. She accepted the former, knowing things do not vanish without cause, and then composed herself. But Heather continued to wander endlessly in a sea of tall grass. "This cannot be right!" she said. "All things must come to an end at some point."

Cumulus clouds hovered in the celestial sky, though the eerie silence gave her the willies. The sun caused poor Heather to break out in a moderate sweat. Luckily, she always carried a bottle of water in her shoulder sack on every trip, in case she got thirsty. She took only one gulp, saving the rest for later, and then proceeded on. Sharp leaves gave her light cuts on her limbs. "Enough!" she said.

Suddenly, a voice from nowhere declared, "Hello there! Are you lost?"

The startled Heather scanned the terrain but came across no one.

"Yoo-hoo! Above you."

Gazing up behind her, she honed in on a talking ear of corn from a stalk that had a frighteningly friendly face. Heather stood there speechless. She tried saying something, but no words would come out of her mouth. *Have I gone mad?* she thought.

"Different, isn't it?" the strange being said to her with a yellow grin.

"Who are you?" she replied in dismay.

"Don't worry, I'm friendly. I just observe from here. In fact, that's all I do. I used to be human like you, but then somehow got trapped in these ears, limiting my domain."

"That's unfortunate! Did you get lost like me?" she asked.

"No. I wasn't really a wanderer. I was a worker at the Hagglehoff Farm years ago until I somehow ended up here. But I cannot remember much of my former self, nor my human name, for that matter. It's a dreadful curse indeed."

"That's sad," Heather said with pity.

"May I ask your name, pretty woman?" the head continued.

"My name is Heather Hazelkind. I teach first grade, and took my students on a field trip to Hagglehoff Farm. But when the wagon opened its iron-gate, I fell into the cornfields. Now I can't seem to find my way out."

"What a pity. That world of yours needs your talent to enlighten the youth and stir them away from trouble."

"Thank you, sir," she said. "But, Mr. Cob—if I may call you that—I need to know where I am. What is this land?"

"No one knows, really. Some say it is part of another dimension, on the outskirts of the universe, perhaps. Others say it is a mysterious fairyland. Yet, others say it might be a psychedelic spell or lucid dream. How we all arrived here is a mystery."

"There are others here as well?" she asked.

"Oh yes, many more in all different sizes, shapes, and forms. My lady, this is not a place that really obeys the laws of nature in your familiar world. This is a land with a plethora of peculiarities, pleasantries, and frightening situations."

"Then can you show me the way out?" she pleaded in earnestness.

"No. There are no signs, roads, or detours of that sort. You can venture in any direction as you please, for everything will eventually merge at the same point. But let me say this: you are bound to encounter many strange things wherever you go— good or bad. If you are fortunate enough, you will leave this place forever. If not, your fate might be oblivion, like me. All I can do for you is comfort you on your journey."

"Then can you follow me all the way through?" she asked him.

"No, for I am cursed and am only granted limited contact with anyone."

Heather nervously gulped over her homeward-bound journey. Pity sank in as she thought of the corn man's woes and hoped she wouldn't end up like him one day. It must have been awfully boring trapped in those ears with hardly anyone to talk to. By then, she almost felt like crying in despair, for her class, the farm, and perhaps the police on the other side who might be looking for her. They might even declare her dead if she couldn't get out. Heather figured if she ever wanted to live to an old age back home, she must make her egress.

"Thank you for your advice, sir. I must be going if I ever want to see my students again."

Gathering her mettle, she departed.

"Be careful, ma'am. Good luck to you!"

"Thank you, sir," she replied.

"God speed, my dear…God speed," the face gravely whispered to himself.

As Heather walked along, she noticed the corn was gradually withering to yellow under the blazing sun. The dirt was hard as rock.

She reached an opening with a haystack in front of a dead, gray tree. Resting a bit on the seat, she took a swig of her water and briefly contemplated her progress before a raspy voice jarred her from her seat.

"Who goes there?" it barked.

Tracing the voice up the ugly tree were two giant crows staring her down. Their wide black eyes were full of death.

"Oh dear. I'm sorry to disturb your lair. I will leave at once," she said.

"Wait!" shouted one of the birds. "We want worms and we want them now! And if you can't find us any, we'll peck your eyeballs out as a substitute. We've done it before!"

Heather felt a chill in her veins. "You can't have my eyeballs," she said. "I'll gladly find you some worms, but you can't have my eyes."

"Very well," said the other crow. "You better find us a pound of them in a half hour. If not, you can go about your business blind!"

"Where can I find worms in this dry climate?" she asked.

"If you look hard enough," said one crow, "you will come across a moist patch of healthy green stalks. From there you will meet a colorful snake we avoid, for fear it might be dangerous. A lot of brightly colored animals are poisonous, you see. It is known to bring out worms, but you must first say these words to summon him:

> *Oh, colorful snake,*
> *Thou warning or fake?*
> *Your stripes a good scare,*
> *So touch not one dare.*
> *Help me, bright snake,*
> *Or poison my fate?*

From that, he might bring out our worms."

Heather rehearsed the silly ditty by rote.

"Okay," she responded.

As Heather exited the opened area, she decided to bolt into the yellow cornfield to lose the birds.

The two crows flew off their perch and pursued her from the air. It wasn't long before they glided past her then broke their stride to peck at her shoulder. The force caused Heather to halt.

"Ouch! That hurt!" she cried out.

"That was just a warning. Next time it will be your eyeballs!" said one crow.

"I'll do what I can!" she said.

"Remember, crows can see better than humans," warned the other bird. And the pair flew back to the dead tree.

Heather surveyed the dry territory. Several minutes elapsed and she still couldn't find the viable patch the wicked crows spoke of.

"Hurry up!" shouted one of the crows from afar.

"I'm trying!" she snapped back. Heather, about to get frustrated, glimpsed a green tinge in her path. Her hope reigniting, she galloped to the sight. Upon her arrival, she thought it bizarre to see a green oasis surrounded by such desolate scenery. The topsoil was indeed rich in water and minerals that nourished the beautiful cornstalks she initially saw.

With relief, she sat down and recited the magic words:

> *Oh, colorful snake,*
> *Thou warning or fake?*
> *Your stripes a good scare,*
> *So touch not one dare.*
> *Help me, bright snake,*
> *Or poison my fate?*

"I'm here, my precious!" declared a voice from below her. Heather looked down to her right and saw a colorful snake coiled around one of the cornstalks. It was normal in size.

"No! I'm here, my precious!"

Another voice spoke from down her left. A similar snake coiled around another stalk.

"You impostor," shouted the snake on the right to its counterpart.

"*You're* the impostor," returned the snake on the left, then addressed her. "Precious, I'm the harmless milk snake, and that is the venomous coral snake."

"You lying scoundrel!" sneered the right snake, then turned to her. "Precious, you have to choose which one of us is the genuine milk snake. If you guess wrong, you must suffer envenomation!"

Heather didn't care for snakes. Her mind zinged back and forth like a pinball machine, for both serpents looked alike as they both had red, black, and yellow stripes, but in a slightly different pattern. One snake had red, black, and yellow stripes respectively, while the other had red, yellow, and black stripes respectively. She thought of not answering but realized the hungry crows would soon be after her.

Suddenly, she remembered an old science teacher she once had who had taught her class a nursery rhyme on how to tell the banded snakes apart.

"Wait!" she exclaimed. "Yellow on black, pay up jack… No, no," she fumbled.

"Yellow to red, you're as good as dead… Maybe… Red to black…something snack, lack. Gosh!" she said, flustered. "Red to yellow…kill a… fellow…" Then Heather's eyes widened.

"I got it!" she said at last. "'Red to yellow, kill a fellow; red to black, venom lack.' You are the milk snake!" She pointed to the right serpent.

"You've done it, my precious!" praised the milk snake.

"Curse your soul, you sharp brute!" bellowed the exasperated coral snake. The defeated serpent vanished.

"Please, Mr. Milk Snake," pleaded Heather. "I need a pound of worms to feed two voracious crows up yonder. If I can't find any, my eyeballs are at stake."

"Oh, I'm aware of those rogues. They're scared of me because I resemble the coral snake—a clever trick indeed. I will retrieve their desire for your sake, only on one condition."

"What's that?" she asked.

"Since I am a milk snake and enjoy the cunning pleasure of sucking milk from cows in their sheds, I will only help you in exchange for some delicious milk."

"That's just a myth," she objected. "The only reason milk snakes venture into cow sheds is to look for mice."

"Nonsense! Not in *this* world," countered the snake. "My offer is my offer."

What luck! Heather felt an immense wave of relief as she remembered the jar of milk in her bag that she'd purchased in the farm shed. She retrieved the milk and fed it to the snake in bewilderment.

The legless critter gulped until satisfied, then exclaimed, "A pound of fresh worms coming up!"

He slithered into a small hole in the soil and brought the worms to her, one after another. "This should be about enough, my dear," he told her after flooding her cupped hands with earthworms.

"Thank you, Mr. Milk Snake," she said, slightly cringing over the slimy night crawlers. She stuffed the annelids into her pockets and headed back toward the dead tree.

Heather placed the worms directly on the haystack altar only to see the repulsive crows devour in greed.

"You can go about your business," dismissed one crow. She left without looking back.

The maize prairies seemed endless, but Heather knew there was an end, since Mr. Cob told her that all paths merged at the same point. She moved steadily and quickly, yet cautiously, fearing danger. By then, Heather's appearance succumbed to grime and leaf scratches.

The corn gradually reverted to its original green color, and the ears whitened. *What illogical microclimate,* she thought to herself.

Feeling a little hungry, Heather thought about eating a raw ear even though she understood it wasn't recommended without it being boiled or grilled. She took a bite from one of them and quickly spat it out, for it was tough, crunchy, and not pleasing to the palate.

A lone grapevine stood in her path.

"Grapes! Great!" she exclaimed and reached for a cluster. Before picking one, the vine mysteriously moved behind one of the leaves to dab the grapes into something. The leaf then rolled itself inward as the tendril uncurled to reveal a glass of red wine.

"Ah, wine! Thank you." Heather took the glass. After drinking, she placed it back onto the grasping tendril and burped. "It's been a long day, and besides, it was just one glass," she reasoned with herself.

Heather looked down the passageway and saw a fat dung beetle a few feet in front of her try to loosen a dung ball wedged against a spiny root with its hind legs.

"Dagnabbit!" it yelled with a tiny voice.

She approached him to help. "Hello there, Dung Beetle. Are you having problems?"

"No. I can manage." The beetle tried and tried again but still couldn't succeed.

Heather stood back and chuckled over his stubborn clumsiness. "Are you sure you don't need any assistance?"

"Okay…I guess I do after all. My wife must be worried by now since I'm delayed getting this ball into the burrow to feed my offspring."

"In that case," she said, "I'll nudge it free with a twig."

"Thank you for your kindness, Ms. Giant."

Heather found a small twig lying around and freed the ball with ease.

"Now, I must reward you for your generosity," said the dung beetle, and he reached his front leg into the core of the dung ball and pulled out a small vial containing a dead iridescent fly. "This is the Luck Fly. I was going to mount it on my wall as a keepsake, but my conscience now tells me I must give it to those I'm thankful for. It is supposed to bring good luck."

Heather took the vial with a red handkerchief she pulled out of her shoulder sack and studied it with interest. The specimen shifted in a spectrum of bright colors. She wrapped the vial in the handkerchief and placed it in her bag, then thanked the dung beetle for his kind generosity.

"Now, I must be on my way. Have a nice day, Ms. Giant."

"You, too."

The dung beetle rolled out of sight.

CHAPTER

2

The arrangement of the cornstalks began to assume an irregular pattern. Instead of neatly defined columns, they spaced themselves widely apart. Then they clustered together. Heather had to weed her way through the tangling mess while more scratches appeared on her limbs.

Later, there were hills to climb. She gritted her teeth and kept going.

While she was prying away a handful of stalks from a small hilltop, she heard a soft voice exclaim, "Oh, brother!"

Off to her side was a destroyed silk web that hung between a leaf blade and a node. A silkworm peeped behind the wreckage and said, "My cocoon is ruined."

"Oh, so sorry, sir," apologized Heather.

"Don't be. It wasn't much of a cocoon, anyway. In fact, I may never become a moth. I build better cocoons if I eat mulberry bushes instead of corn. The reason I am in a cornfield is because a wicked crow snatched me from my home by the brook where wild mulberry bushes grow. While in flight, the crow dropped me by accident, and I ended up here."

Heather thought for a moment about the silkworm's plight before suggesting, "Perhaps I can take you along with me, so I can try to find your home."

"That would please me very much, Ms....?"

"Heather. Heather Hazelkind."

"Thank you, Heather. May I ride inside your shoulder sack on the way?"

"Certainly, Mr. Silkworm." Heather bundled the critter into her bag along with a few leaves to make a nice niche for him to burrow in. Then on she went.

CHAPTER
3

Eventually the ground flattened to a dirt corridor flanked by two fields. The left field was bright green, while the right field was robbed of much of its color.

Heather hastened down the corridor before an uncomely voice startled her to a halt.

"Surrender now! You can't defeat us! We are greener than you. The brook is ours!"

She traced the voice to a talking ear from the green side. They all had faces. Additionally, every stalk had their fibrous roots freed for mobility. Their cornhusks resembled helmets and their leaf blades yielded toward their opponents like swords.

"This must be a standoff!" Heather quietly hid.

"We will never yield to you!" countered another ear from the discolored side. "We tire from living in places that deny us water while you greedy green grasses seek more! The brook is rightfully ours and we will fight gallantly for it!"

"Then so be it!" spat the green colonel. "Charge!"

The two armies engaged. Their blades sliced through their opponents like warm knives in butter.

Plant appendages hurled about in all directions: ears, leaves, nodes, roots. Amazed at how sharp the blades were, Heather cringed at the thought of them contacting flesh. The violent mishap reminded her of the lessons she gave to her little pupils about the horrors of the American Civil War. It was one of the most grueling wars in U.S. history. Americans fought Americans, where soldiers lost limbs from guns, cannons, and bayonets. Many underwent painful amputations before the advent of anesthetics. Fortunately, these plants felt no pain as they lacked nerves—they fell apart like jigsaw puzzle pieces.

The battle of the cornstalks lasted until hardly any remained. Neither side won. Those fortunate to survive either ran home or persisted toward the brook. All in all, the whole territory was a wasteland.

"See what happens when all reason fails," spoke a voice from behind her. Heather turned around but found no one. It sounded like Mr. Cob she met early on, but he was nowhere in sight. Heather had no choice but to move forward, stepping over scattered debris in hopes of the foretold brook ahead. The water promised the chance to refresh herself.

Somewhere around noon, the corn became massive and sturdy like resin. They towered like redwood trees. Heather felt like an ant wandering through a gigantic garden. Shade finally relieved her from the savage sun.

Drinking the last of her bottled water, she held onto the bottle to refill it with water from the brook. The moist, dark soil gradually became sandier with rocks and pebbles sprinkled about, indicating a body of water nearby. The land also had bracken.

Within moments, she spotted a sparkling stream two yards wide with a gentle flow. As she approached it, she could see that the crystal-clear water housed beautiful carp that added to the water's gleam. A lovely setting it was, she thought.

A row of wild mulberry bushes sat along the banks, housing numerous silk cocoons populated with their larval inhabitants. She opened her shoulder sack, informed her passenger of his homecoming, and placed the silkworm into his natural dwelling. The silkworm greeted his fellow neighbors with much merriment, as they thought he wouldn't return.

"Oh, I am in debt to you, my savior heroine!" he told her gleefully. "If there is anything I could do for you I would gladly do it. Hmm…let me see… ah, yes! If you could stash as many mulberry leaves into your sack as possible, I could spin you a nice thick, silk coat for your journey, before I cocoon into a moth. You may need it." Heather obliged. The silkworm parted with his peers for the last time, and back into the shoulder sack the silkworm went.

A giant object brushed passed her face. Startled, Heather looked around before noticing a giant butterfly perched onto a great corn stump in the background.

"Don't look at it," a voice called from her side. A frantic old woman, who looked to be in her seventies, came running after her. "Its enchanting beauty will steal your eyes if you look at it too long."

Heather realized the old woman's gray face had empty eye-sockets.

"Here! Put these on, for they shield its magic." The old woman handed her a pair of round sunglasses.

Gazing up at the creature in polarized light, Heather noticed that the butterfly didn't look like ordinary butterflies, but in fact was intimidating in bulk and appearance. Its large wings had dark hues of purple, red, and magenta, like the birefringence from gasoline. The black body was hefty and neatly lineated through the muscles, although it still retained a feminine physique. A towering crown of antennae and pink, almond-shaped eyes looked formidable.

"Look at its eyespots," the eyeless woman told her. Heather found that each of the butterfly's hind wings had a distinct circle with a black center and a light blue periphery, like an iris.

"Those are my eyes. That mimicking beast! Now I can only see from the butterfly's perspective," said the old woman.

Heather sympathized with the old lady for making her way with such distorted vision. "It's a good thing I have the whole terrain memorized, and I can still feel," added the nice woman.

Heather then decided to negotiate with the poor old lady's adversary to see if she could peacefully get the woman's eyes back. "Please, Ms. Butterfly," she said. "Could you kindly give this poor woman her eyes back? Your wings are still beautiful without them."

"What color are your eyes?" the butterfly replied in a raspy, feminine voice.

"Brown," she responded.

"Hmm. Since these blue ones don't exactly match my coloration, I shall take yours in exchange for hers!" asserted the wicked monarch butterfly.

"You can't have my eyes," Heather said. "I've been over this topic before."

"Very well," decided the creature. "I shall take them by force!"

The disturbed insect swooped down to forcefully remove Heather's sunspecs. Wings violently thrashed about her face, picking up wind and dust, as the scary legs picked at her shades. Heather screamed and wildly flung her arms to fend off the beast.

Eventually, the fiend wrapped her menacing limbs around Heather's face, with Heather's hands pinned in between the two of them.

Using all her other senses, the old woman picked up a log at the last moment and swatted the ugly butterfly from Heather's face.

The insect retreated to the tall stump in fury. "I won't stop till I get those browns!" she shouted.

"I must have my eyes back! How are we going to defeat that filthy animal?" the lady said to Heather, who was panting.

"Do you know anything about that thing?" Heather asked her.

"Yes," the old woman said. "The wicked butterfly was once a beautiful pixie that fell in love with her image so much that she was mysteriously cursed into becoming a mad butterfly. She robbed the eyes of those who looked upon her thereafter in order to decorate her wings."

Heather paused until a clever thought entered her mind. Whispering into the old lady's ear, she asked, "Do you have a large mirror?"

The old woman brightened. "I sure do, my brainy child. I'll be back." She scampered into the giant forest again.

A moment later, she rolled out a full-length swivel mirror with the dull side facing the butterfly.

"All right, you narcissist! Here's your medicine!" shouted the old lady.

The two women swung the mirror around, reflecting the butterfly's spooky image. Her eyespots glowed and left their place in midair to peruse the reflection. Enraged over being outwitted by the two women, the butterfly flew into position to block the eyespots' path, but the creature's wings were too translucent to prevent the eyespots from seeing her mirrored self, and so they continued their course. The women laughed in triumph.

Once stuck to the mirror, the eyespots transformed back into pretty blue eyeballs. The old lady laughed in glee once more as she carefully picked them off and positioned them back into her sockets, shading her eyes.

"You have been defeated, my cunning queen," she snickered at the beast. "Now we know how to break your spell."

The monarch gave one last angry howl and flew off.

"Missy, you're a lifesaver," the old woman spoke to Heather as they both unshaded their eyes. "If America had gotten rid of their monarchs then why can't we?" she joked. "May I ask your name?"

"Heather Hazelkind. And yours?"

"Margaret Dune. Have you gotten lost in this land, dearie?"

"Yes," Heather said. "Well, sort of, I guess."

"Don't worry. I've heard it doesn't go on forever, as it may seem. Although, I haven't had the energy to explore it all."

Heather noticed Margaret was wearing a ruby ladybug pendant the size of a half-dollar, threaded by a thin cerulean ribbon. Her sweet tenderness reflected its charm.

"Anyways, I'd be more than happy to do anything you'd like, since you spared a terrible burden on a tired old woman."

Just then, Heather's stomach growled. "Well, I am a little hungry…"

"Oh, then you're just in time for tea. Come now."

The old lady led Heather a short distance into the giant corn forest where they came across a well. Margaret unclamped a short rope that supported a wooden bucket dangling from the wheel and axel and set it aside. She then reached into a sack on the side of the well to obtain a pillow-sized teabag with a rope clamp. She clamped the bag onto the well rope and rotated the axel to lower it.

Kooky! Heather thought.

"This will take some time, so let's get our honey cakes," said Margaret Dune. "Go pick me some tulips and tassels over there." She pointed toward a garden wire fence that nursed pretty flowers and baby corn. Heather stepped over the fence and began to pick the tulips and male corn flowers.

"Don't pick the red ones. The bees can't see in red," informed Margaret.

"What bees?" Heather asked.

"They can see yellow and everything else in a pretty purple," the little lady added.

"Are you all right, Miss Dune?"

"Of course, silly girl," swiftly returned Dune.

"But aren't bees dangerous?" Heather asked.

"No, no. Not these ones. I exchange pollen and nectar with them for yummy honey cakes they make. A friendly bunch they are, at least to me."

Heather nervously continued to pick violet and yellow tulips with the tassels. Completed, she headed back to Margaret, where a beekeeping veil was presented to her. "Put this on and stand behind me, for they don't know you yet."

Heather felt a little uneasy at this statement and quickly veiled her face.

"Are you ready?" asked Margaret.

"If you insist. Although I can't see how a butterfly can be more dangerous than bees."

The old lady chuckled. "All righty then. Follow me."

They wandered into the humongous forest until they spotted a fuzzy honeybee the size of a mouse fly over and perch itself on a giant leaf blade. "Who goes there!" it snapped with a biting little voice.

"Have no fear, Margaret Dune is here," replied the little woman with confidence.

"Oh, Margaret! I almost didn't recognize you," replied the bee that sounded female.

"Yes, it's me, Dixi 9. How are things going with the colony?"

"Not too well, Margaret," confessed the bee. "The queen is worried since most of my sisters have disappeared. There is no telling about their whereabouts."

"That's strange!" said Dune. "Is it okay if I see the queen?"

"Who's that?" Dixi 9 shifted her attention to Heather.

"She's a friend of mine under that veil. Don't worry, she's not a honey thief."

"Sorry if I'm being a little uptight. It's been a long couple of days," said Dixi. "The queen will especially like the nice flowers you have there, Margaret. You can follow me."

Dixi 9 led the party in a steady, lazy flight to the bees' lair. Brushing away the last leaf in front of her, Heather beheld a meticulously designed beehive hanging from a giant maize branch. It hung at head-level and was the size of a dog house. The honeycombs were molded into a palace with pillars, plazas, verandas, balconies, tiers, and many rooms. However, welcoming though it was, it was nearly vacant.

Heather heard faint weeping coming from inside.

"Wait here," said Dixi 9, and flew into the hive by way of a comb balcony. Her voice floated out as she spoke to someone inside. "Royal Mother, Margaret Dune is here with some pretty yellow flowers."

Halting her sorrow for the moment, the queen spoke up in a low, tender voice, "Oh, how nice of her to console me in such dismal times. Bring her forward."

"You can come now!" called the servant bee to the women.

Margaret assured Heather it was safe to remove her face protection upon approach. The balcony unlatched as Dixi 9 pushed it open. The ladies saw a cozy, plush room with a fat bee the size of a rat lying on a tiny sofa made of beeswax. She was crowned in a wreath of flower anthers.

Margaret peered into the room and gently asked, "How are you faring, Queen Nonabi?"

"Unfortunately, not too well Margaret. Many of my daughters have vanished."

"So I heard," said Dune.

"It's a shame that we have such a beautiful home and hardly anyone around anymore. I don't think I angered them into deserting me. Do you suppose they were captured? Or worse, do you think they all went mad and died of disease? My poor workers…" The queen began to sob again.

"Don't think of any bad thoughts," Margaret told the queen. "They will just make you feel worse."

"I know. But I stopped laying eggs out of grief. Now, I don't know whether my colony will make it or not."

The few remaining bees also began to weep. Margaret and Heather began to feel somewhat dispirited as well.

"What a pity," Margaret said.

"I have been sensing a mysterious change in the cornfields lately," continued the queen bee.

"That's interesting," added Margaret. "I, too, have sensed malaise from Maizeland. It all feels devoid of love."

Heather listened.

"Whatever it is, my poor daughters were probably taken away by it. Without them, a new queen cannot be reared in my stead after I depart."

"Don't fret, my kind queen," soothed Margaret. "It's hard to imagine your kind of such number and beauty to vanish."

"Thank you," sobbed the queen. She looked at Heather. "Who's that?"

"This is a nice friend of mine named Heather Hazelkind."

"Please to meet you, Ms. Hazelkind. You and Margaret look like twins, if you disregard the age gap."

Heather smiled.

"Dixi 9, would you take those flowers from Margaret," asked the queen bee.

Dixi 9 flew over to take the colorful bouquet from Margaret's hands. She laid them beside the queen.

"What a marvelous yellow. Thank you so much, Margaret. These will especially help in making the delicious honey cakes," said Queen Nonabi.

"Oh, I know!" added the little woman.

"Would you and your friend like some for tea?" the queen courteously asked.

"That would be nice if it isn't that much trouble for you."

"Not at all. There is plenty of honey left over. Please take some."

Dixi 9 flew into a special room and drew out a plate made of beeswax with moist cornbread sweetened with the bees' special honey. Margaret took the plate and smiled.

"Thank you," she said to the queen. "We must have our lunch now. I hope your workers return, Your Majesty."

"That would be wonderful," returned the mother bee.

Margaret curtsied to the royal insect, followed by Heather. The two women headed back toward the well with the bread.

"I feel sorry for the queen," commented Heather.

"I do too," said Margaret. "The mood doesn't seem right here anymore. My husband and I liked this beautiful, magic land for the nice shade, plentiful fish, and our friends. Even if it seems odd, we'd planned to die here."

"Where is your husband?" asked Heather.

"He passed away recently."

"Oh, I'm sorry." She sympathized with her loneliness.

"No need to feel sorry for me. We all face death at some point. As long as there are no regrets or hurt feelings, good memories will keep us happy for a long time." Mrs. Dune spoke with wisdom. "Now, let's get our tea!"

Handing over the honey-bread, she cranked the axel in reverse, which wound the rope up the well. Instead of seeing a large wetted tea bag surface, a harnessed saucer with a teacup set reared from the depths. Mrs. Dune giggled, but Heather was flabbergasted.

"Splendid!" Dune said, unharnessing the set. "Let's dine."

Margaret led Heather to the widest giant cornstalk not too far from the stream. An inconspicuous door from the tree trunk was seen. There were even subtle stories of windows.

Upon entering, a bird chirped from a small wooden birdhouse that hung on one of the home's great leaf shoots.

Mrs. Dune approached it. "Oh, Birdie, I see your clutch has hatched!"

"All but one," a warbler said, peeping out of the hole. "That cuckoo is at it again."

"Oh!" exclaimed Mrs. Dune. "Has she been laying in your nest again?"

"Every time I'm gone! Why does she do that, Margaret? It's very selfish of her!" The birdhouse nested a few chicks lying around a larger egg with gray spots instead of brown. "Once it's out and about, it will probably hog up all the food from my poor children. I've learned how to spot one by now. Should I try to push it off the treehouse?"

"No need," said Mrs. Dune. "I'll take it and rear it myself."

Heather thought, *What a nice lady.*

"Why don't you fry it up, Margaret? That will give her something to think about," suggested the warbler with a grin.

"I don't have the heart for that. If she ever comes close to my window, I might have a talk with her on how to be a better mom."

"Good luck with that!" said the bird.

"Here, have some honey-cake for you and your brood." Margaret tore off a piece and gave it to the birds in exchange for the cuckoo egg.

"Thanks Margaret. Queen Nonabi sure makes the best cornbread in all of Maizeland."

"She sure does." Into the peculiar home Mrs. Dune and Heather went.

Some of the inside furnishings where made from maize. Mrs. Dune placed the estranged egg in a shoebox with leaf paper to incubate it. The women chatted and gossiped like good-time friends during and after their nice luncheon. Through the conversation, Heather understood that Mrs. Dune was unable to have children in her younger years and her whole family was gone. She had once been a teacher of botany and enjoyed being around the plants. In fact, she owned a greenhouse. Heather received a small lesson that the wide girth of the giant cornstalks was to tolerate gravity and their wide spacing was to minimize root crowding, just like tall redwood trees.

Heather told Mrs. Dune a little about herself, too. Heather was born to Jed and Kate Hazelkind. Her father was a persistent salesman and her mother was a good cook and seamstress. Her father worked hard to put his little girl through college for her to become what she always wanted—a great teacher. Unfortunately, he died from his dreadful habit of smoking. Her mother had lost one of her legs to cancer and mostly confined herself to a wheelchair before getting a wooden leg. Heather, feeling sorrow for her family's misfortune, vowed never to take her folks for granted again as she once had in a bout of teenage rebellion.

When she was sixteen, she dismissed her mother's knitting lessons because she thought they were for old ladies, not realizing it was a selfish way to fracture a traditional bond with her mother.

Another time, Heather wanted to buy an expensive hat for the summer because some of her friends were wearing it and she asked her father for money. He refused because he felt she could work to earn the money for the hat. She resented that idea. The next day, Heather's father asked her to drop off mail at the post office because his back was aching from all the sales he'd worked to make over the week and her mother was teaching sewing downtown. While she set out to the post office, she discovered her father had cash in one of the envelopes for a church tithe. She secretly took out the cash and bought the expensive hat. When her father found out about it later, there was a big family argument. She had betrayed his trust.

Those were the days she disliked the most.

As an adult, she visited her mother as much as possible and happily participated in activities with her, including embroidery and cooking, since that was the only family she had left. She would speak to her father in prayer almost every night and would gladly volunteer in her church over the weekends.

Heather was about to marry, but the man she thought she loved didn't treat her with much respect, the way a true gentleman should.

Mrs. Dune played music from a gramophone record player that had a large hedge bindweed flower for a horn. New Orleans jazz back in the Roaring Twenties was her favorite, especially "Black Bottom

Stomp" by Jelly Roll Morton. She gave Heather
swing dance lessons and they laughed in joy together.

As time went by, Heather spotted a fishing rod
made of sturdy cornstalk leaning against a wall. It
was threaded with strong string that had a small hook

tied to the end. Fishing with her late father brought back warm memories.

"It's almost dinnertime, Mrs. Dune, and I must be on my way soon. May I borrow your fishing rod to fish for those giant carp outside?" she asked.

"Please, be my guest, my child. Oh, before you go, I want to give you something." The old woman removed her ladybug necklace to give to her.

"Oh, I can't take that," Heather said humbly.

"Take it, my dear. I wore it long enough. You're a lady like me now. The spots on the left wing represent seven sorrows, while the spots on the right wing represent seven joys."

Heather studied the red wings in her hand and found one black spot on the right wing. She figured that that spot must have represented her joy with Mrs. Dune.

"Remember me by it," the old woman requested.

"I will," Heather assured her, and wore it over her heart before leaving.

"One more thing," cautioned Mrs. Dune before she left. "Be careful at dusk, for I have heard there is something mad lurking out in the fields."

Heather froze for a moment, wondering what she meant by that. "Thanks for the advice."

Mrs. Dune was like a grandmother to Heather, for she never knew her real grandparents who died before her birth.

CHAPTER

4

Refilling her water bottle in the sparkly stream, Heather seated herself on a giant ear log, watching the heavenly fish swim by. Heather wished she had a camera to take pictures for her class.

"Hello again, Ms. Hazelkind," greeted Mr. Cob, the log on which she sat. A few of the kernels were chipped out from his nose and lips.

"Hello again, Mr. Cob," she returned, bending over to him.

"What have you learned on your adventure?" he asked.

"Lots. It's lovely around here, but Nature can be very dangerous at times."

"Good observation," he remarked.

Heather continued, "Mrs. Dune is a very nice lady. Though, I can't fully understand why she would stay here all alone, without anyone else of her kind."

"Some prefer just that," said the ear. "Both worlds have their own ups and downs. Whichever one you're comfortable with is all that matters."

"I guess that makes sense," Heather said. "The bees have nearly vanished. What troubles this land?"

"I guess you'll have to find that out for yourself," he said.

"In any case, how much more do I have left of this place? I'm getting a little tired, and I miss my job and family," she said.

"I cannot say to be sure, Ms. Hazelkind," he stated.

"Well fine, if that's the way you feel, then so be it!" she uttered impatiently.

His large face quickly receded. "I must be off, but I will check on you from time to time."

"Wait, Mr. Cob! I didn't mean to offend you like that."

No reply.

"Darn it!" She pouted after feeling childish over her poor choice of conduct.

Winding down, she asked herself, "What am I going to use for bait?"

When looking around, she heard a gentle ringing noise, like that of a tuning fork, from her shoulder sack. She opened it to look inside and found that it was coming from the vial she'd gotten from the dung beetle. When she unwound the handkerchief covering the vial, the dead insect glowed intensely as it rang.

"The Luck Fly!" she exclaimed. "Is it telling me something? Does it want me to use it for bait?"

Heather washed the vial in the clear water before removing the glowing specimen. She took a chance and decided to hook and cast the fly into the water. Immediately, she felt a tug from the stream's bottom. It nearly yanked the pole out from her hands. Suddenly, a slimy form broached the water and landed in her arms. Once the splashing abated, she realized she was holding a fat, queer fish with a face that looked oddly human, as it had diamond blue eyeballs and jumbo lips in the shape of a smile. Gold scales gilded the body.

A boyish voice spoke up to her, "You caught me with the Luck Fly, did you not?"

"Yes," Heather said.

"I'm the only one who eats the Luck Fly. My name is Lempet, the Golden Carp. My scales are made of real gold."

Heather examined the creature's body and confirmed it to be true.

"What is your name?" asked the strangeling.

"Heather Hazelkind."

"Please to meet you, Ms. Hazelkind. You must be special. I will thank you for the Luck Fly lunch by rewarding you, if you let me go. Unhook me, if you please."

"But where will you take me?" she asked.

"You'll find that out if you just unhook me and follow wherever I go."

Heather, hesitant to oblige out of questionable trust, unhooked the strange creature and placed him back into the crystal water.

"Follow the leader," Lempet called from the surface, and off she went.

CHAPTER

5

As she walked along the banks, the sandy soil became grassy. Wind picked up, and the corn trees began to twitch. A giant ear of corn landed unexpectedly to Heather's left, causing a big clamor that shook the ground.

"Watch your step, Heather," warned Lempet. "It's quite unstable around here."

"Definitely," she said. Tiptoeing with caution, she thought, *What if it had landed on someone like me?*

Heather soon came to a grassy clearing with a ring of squat mushrooms called a fairy ring. The grass inside this circle was paler, since the soil nutrients were being drawn by the mushrooms. Heather stepped into the ring to admire its circular appeal.

Realizing where Heather was standing, Lempet called from the waterfront, "Uh-oh! Madam, get out of there!"

But it was too late; Heather couldn't move. The cap of each mushroom began to form a talking mouth. The fungi hideously laughed with eerie, pearly white teeth. The lead mushroom in front of her spoke.

"You walked inside the fairy ring, Missy. Now you must answer three questions. If you get any wrong, you shall rot in your place for twenty years and become our substrate!" They all laughed in concert.

"Are you ready?" it asked.

Pressed, Heather responded with an anxious, "Okay. What now?"

"All right, number one: what is the name of the farm from your world?"

"That would be Hagglehoff Farm," she answered with ease.

"Great Job, Heather!" Lempet shouted.

"Number two," the head mushroom started again. "Are ravens and crows the same?"

"Hmm…" Heather thought for a moment to reason her way out of the question. She had seen these birds in books before and tried to size them up in her head. After a little recollection, she responded, "No."

"How so?" smugly returned the mushroom.

With a little more thought, Heather answered, "Ravens are bigger."

"Bravo, my lass. Bravo!" exclaimed Lempet.

The mushrooms pouted.

"And now…heh, heh…for number three: what are the colors of the Luck Fly?"

This was the most difficult question of them all. There were many colors it emitted, like the rainbow.

Wait! she thought. *The rainbow, that's it!* "Roy G. Biv," she said, remembering another mnemonic device from her old science teacher. "R for red, O for orange, Y for yellow, G for green, B for blue, I for indigo, and V for violet."

The mushrooms roared in anger.

"You did it, my lady, you've won!" Lempet cheered.

Relieved, she sighed and stepped out of the ring. The roaring stopped upon her exit, as the mushrooms resumed their natural form again.

"Let's go!" Lempet said with spirit. Strangely enough, she began to like the fish for his faith and support in her. They made good friends. Lempet later teased her on the fact that had she answered incorrectly, he would have had to summon Mrs. Dune to destroy the mushrooms around her to free her from their grasp.

The evening dimmed the sky as the landscape changed again. The vast great cornstalks grew gnarly, like weeds sprawling out in distress. Some were very large, and others were normal in size. Vein-like prop roots webbed the foggy ground that eroded to mud.

These plants were largely dull, grayish brown, and the ears were likely inedible. Weeds, thorny shrubs, and some hideous trees were everywhere she walked. The once clear, thirst-quenching brook was a murky river one could hardly see through. The land before her gave her a creepy feeling.

She walked in her sullied shoes and declared, "I don't like this place; I want to go back right now." She faced Lempet, but an even stranger fish was seen lurking alongside her. "Goodness! Who are you? Where is Lempet?" she exclaimed.

"It's still me, Heather," it spoke in a more mature voice. She noticed it gulping air while talking. This creature resembled an electric eel, except that the head had a wide sucker-mouth instead of jaws of needle teeth, and its eyes were not acute but round and friendly.

"Lempet?" she questioned in awe.

"Yes, it's me. The water is somewhat poor in oxygen, so I transformed into a lungfish."

"Your voice has changed," she said.

"That's because I have a different voice box now," the lungfish explained.

"Your eyes have changed," she continued, noticing them as brown instead of blue.

"That's because they can now blend in with the water," he replied.

"Weird, but clever," she remarked. "Where are you taking me, Lempet? I don't like this place."

"I'm taking you to my master, Crempet, the Great Catfish," he answered.

"Why?"

"You may be able to receive the mud pearl."

"What's that?" she asked.

"You'll see. Come along."

Heather followed him onward through the eerie forest.

CHAPTER

6

The party approached a black pond. "The catfish resides in that pool up yonder, Heather. From him, you might be able to obtain the sacred mud pearl if you pass the test."

"Why so many tests?" she asked.

"Don't worry, this is a good test, unlike with the mushrooms. It's a test of virtue. You must seek him at once, for he's expecting you. I have to go now, but I might be around later on. It was nice meeting you." Lempet left her in the gloom to return to the brook as a goldfish.

"Wait!" she called out, but he was gone. The silence gave her the creeps, as one could easily hear a pin drop. She hoped this wasn't a trap.

A mild chill crept up her back, and she opened her shoulder sack in the dark. "Have you made my silk coat yet, Mr. Silkworm?"

"Not yet, my gracious," he said with a grin, entangled in silk mesh. She closed the bag and grumbled a little.

In due time, bubbles surfaced the shore until a huge, grimy body emerged. Small black eyes appeared from the sides of a colossal head. Huge pointy whiskers arose, and below them was a giant mouth that gaped wide open, capable of swallowing a person.

"Hello, Ms. Hazelkind," the catfish greeted her in a bass voice. "You have been selected to seek the mud pearl."

"Yes, I guess so," she answered.

"Be prepared for examination, for only the truly virtuous will behold the mysterious powers of the mighty pearl. Are you ready to take the test?"

"For what?" she asked.

"You can help us all."

"Well, where is it?" she inquired.

"Crawl inside my magic belly, for there resides the artifact."

"What?" she said, sure she had misunderstood him. "You're trying to trick me for a meal, aren't you?"

"Trust me, Heather," Crempet calmly replied. Heather felt a strange, welcoming compulsion toward the fish's giant mouth.

She sighed. "My purse is filled with knitting needles, you know."

The catfish giggled and said, "You have my word."

She carefully stepped onto the slippery jaw.

"Don't worry, it's easy," assured Crempet. "It will be like swallowing a turkey—just kidding."

Heather sighed once more and then crouched into his slimy mouth. Queasiness fell upon her as she smelled dead fishes laced in pondweed.

"Don't burp on me, all right?" she told him.

The catfish gave one loud belch that blew her hair backwards and then chuckled again.

"That's it, I'm out of here," she declared while getting ready to step out.

"Wait!" Crempet replied. "I was just teasing you. I'm done now, please come back."

Heather hesitated, then climbed back in. Suddenly, the jaws clamped shut and she felt a submergence from the upward force of her inertia. The jaws opened once more to invite a flood of water into the huge mouth. Heather, soaked from head to toe, was swiftly gulped down into an unknown realm. It was terrifying.

She floated in a colorful dreamscape with a gentle breeze and felt dry and light. Peace was all around her and she quickly felt at ease. A boggy clamshell then faded into view and a majestic voice boomed from inside it.

"Who seeks me out?"

She answered. "Heather Hazelkind."

"Come forth and place your hand on my shell."

Heather did as the voice decreed and felt strange warmth coming from the bivalve.

She was pulled into a trance where time seemed irrelevant. Everything happened all at once, yet it felt like time could stretch and shrink at will.

Heather saw a visual sequence of her life go by starting from her birth to her present. Certain events were quickly passed over, but other events were slowed down and emphasized with great detail. She relived these experiences by feeling both her emotions as well as those of whom she'd interacted with. Five memories were brought to her attention with great emphasis.

The first memory was when Heather was ten years old and a flash flood had hit her town in Nebraska. That night, the rain and flood water had been so intense that Heather's father asked her and her mother to help him set up camp on the roof of the house inside a tent. The weather cleared up early the next morning and the water was calm, though it was still overcast with slight drizzle. Heather heard meowing in a stranded tree at a distance while her parents still slept, and she used her father's raft he'd assembled the night before and paddled her way to the tree. Heather saved an old cat that readily jumped on board with her. She then heard barking and spotted a white terrier dog stranded on a storage tank that was mostly covered in water. The dog readily jumped on board, too. By then her father had awakened and seen what she was doing. Heather further saved a rabbit, mouse, and raccoon.

When she arrived back to the roof of the house with her rescued friends, her father smiled and said, "I'm very proud of you, Heather. Just tell me next time you are going to do something like that, okay? I love you, pumpkin."

"I love you too, Daddy," she replied. The animals were fed from the family's food storage and sheltered until the water receded the next day.

Her next memory was from high school. There was a spoiled girl who felt entitled to bully other girls she felt were inferior to her, particularly one who was overweight and lacked self-esteem. One school night, Heather was the last to leave the gym after the school's basketball team's winning game and caught the snotty girl, in the company of her superficial friends, sticking copies of drawings on hallway lockers depicting an exaggeration of the overweight girl. These pictures read, "Help me, I'm fat!"

They left, thinking no one saw them. Heather took all the pictures down and threw them in the trash before the next school day. She then saw the bully enter the girl's bathroom the next day with her friends. Heather marched in where they were gossiping about the poor, overweight girl, planning what they were going to do next to her, and Heather confronted the bully about the pictures. The girl told Heather to shut up and mind her business and Heather refused. She pushed Heather, and Heather pushed back. The girls engaged in a tussle and

Heather bested her in the end. As they calmed down, Heather told the aggressor that her actions had murdered the overweight girl in her heart and that she should learn to feel how others are treated for once. After that incident, the bully never put down anyone again.

In her third memory, Heather was working in a convalescent home to pay her rent as well as her teaching credential program. A ninety-year-old woman she was preparing meals for had never felt so appreciative toward her, as her long-deceased husband had been a drunk and her two sons were too busy getting rich and snooty to pay her any attention. Heather acted as the feeble woman's daughter she'd never had. She celebrated holidays with her, sang to her, gave her makeovers, and made sure she never felt lonely. Heather was very sad when the old woman passed away but knew that however short her time was with her, the lady died happily in the end.

Her next memory took place after she had begun teaching. Heather had a talented student in her class one year, but he cried the week after the first semester because his mother expected him to get perfect grades on his report card and his father was disappointed that he had struck out in farm league baseball, losing a game. Heather scheduled a conference with the boy's parents and they weren't too receptive of her at first, but then they listened to her.

"You know," she said, "life isn't about getting perfect scores or hitting homeruns all the time.

School is about learning, and sports are about having fun. Your love for your son is more important than trying to make him into the next Edward Teller or Jackie Robinson. You don't want to jeopardize your relationship with him over material things. You should love your son the way he is, regardless, and give him lots of encouragement."

The parents left without saying a word, but then came back after the next semester and deeply thanked her for her considerable wisdom. Their relationship with their son markedly improved because they took her advice, and they were a happier family from then on.

In her last memory, Heather was visiting her father in the hospital for the last time. His final words to her before he slipped into a coma and passed away were, "Heather, my time on earth is coming to an end. I wish I could continue to see you grow, but I am being called to a higher place. I will always be with you. I know I wasn't always the best father at times but remember the good things I taught you and pass them on for generations to come."

Heather sobbed with her mother and kissed him while holding his hand. "I will," she promised.

"I love you, pumpkin," he said feebly.

"I love you too, Daddy."

And then he was gone.

Before a tear could fall from her eye, Heather was pulled out of the trance and heard bells pealing in the background.

The clam grandly proclaimed, "Thou hath won the mud pearl, child. Taketh and secure it with care."

Its upper shell abducted to reveal a dull pearl rested on the foot. Heather took it in wonder and it shimmered ethereally in her hand upon contact.

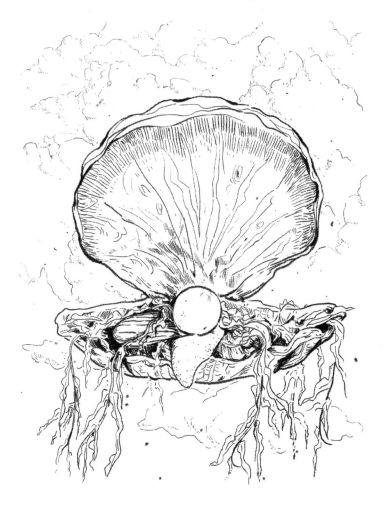

"Thy pearl's secret shall be revealed to you on your last stop. Keep it at hand and entrust it to none."

The shell adducted, and Heather found herself forced out of the mouth of the great catfish onto the shore again, as if time had rewound itself.

"Congratulations Heather," Crempet bid farewell and re-submerged into the black pond.

"What was that?" she asked herself, feeling damp but not soaked. She stared at the magic mud pearl again with fascination before safely placing it into a secret compartment in her shoulder sack. It was nearly pitch-black outside and she laboriously walked through the alluvium.

A faint rummaging noise came through the gnarly shrubs behind her. A chill moved through her as the shuffling became more apparent. From the dark shadows peered a lifeless face into the moonlight. The eyeless scarecrow she had first seen on her adventure arrived in her presence on foot. Its eye sockets were as black as a shark's, its expressionless face was gaunt, and the worn clothing implied a sense of cold neglect, for it was discolored and threadbare. The dry corn leaf stuffing protruded out of the loose seams of the stitched body, like Medusa snakes. The sewn face stared her down as if it were scowling but she couldn't tell what emotions the scarecrow had, if any. It was a cold stare with no personality, no sign of humanity. The whole character was like a dark void with no hope of light.

Raising a sickle out of the darkness, the towering humanoid growled at her in a hoarse voice, "I want your head!"

Heather shrieked and ran for her life. The creature pursued her, weeding his way through the debris with the baneful weapon. His smiting strength was immense for a stuffed scarecrow. She started to cry and then tripped in the mud. With a burst of energy, she flung herself off the icky ground and continued to run with all her might as the swiping of debris neared her.

She yelled frantically, tearing her way through the briars that scratched her hands until a trace of light was seen ahead. Fortunately, the ground hardened just in time as she saw a small campfire on the way. Darting into the encircled arena, she looked back to find no trace of the scarecrow.

"What troubles you, miss?" a soft voice spoke from the campfire.

She turned and saw a headless woman seated on a lounge chair. Gasping in horror, she discovered other headless bodies seated around the fire. They were all normally clothed.

"A mad scarecrow is after me!" she exclaimed.

"My goodness, poor child! He won't bother you now, for scarecrows are afraid of fire. Come, sit in this chair, you're probably cold by now."

Another lounge chair sat close to the lady figure, and Heather, though hesitant to trust these eerie beings, sat in it to further avoid the scarecrow and to calm herself down and warm up. They even handed her a coarse blanket. The campfire heated a medium-sized cauldron hung on a tripod holder. She hoped they weren't cooking something human inside. The flames were so warm, though, that Heather did not want to budge from her seat for a long time.

"What is your name, dear?" the lady creature asked in a soft voice that resonated from her neck stump.

"Heather Hazelkind."

"What a lovely name. Are you hungry?"

"Yes," Heather replied shyly.

"Then you can pick some potatoes below you and toss them into the pot. There is also fresh corn and lima beans behind you. These should give you enough sustenance for the night."

Heather looked down and yanked a small potato shrub from its roots, which revealed the fat tubers. She then saw a few green cornstalks behind her that ironically bore healthy cobs. Beside it was a lima bean bush. She picked almost every edible part and threw them into the cauldron.

"I'm Sally Breen," the woman figure said. "And beside me is my husband, Bobby." A skinny body sat next to the lady. "And those two are Percy and Lilly Forst." Two headless heavy-set couples sat farther down and greeted her kindly. These people mysteriously sensed her presence without eyes or ears.

"How did you find your way up here?" Sally Breen asked.

Heather explained her whole journey starting from the farm.

"You've come a long way, my dear," acknowledged Bobby Breen afterward. Heather felt more comfortable around the bodies, even if they seemed rather scary at first.

"Dinner's ready," announced Percy. They prepared Heather a plate of two warm corn-on-the-cobs with a baked potato and soft lima beans. They even had butter to go around! She thanked them for their kind hospitality and thought, *How could these people eat without heads?* Looking up at them, she confirmed they weren't eating at all.

The headless people chuckled. "We don't eat, my dear, for we died a long time ago," Sally explained.

"We are ghosts called 'the headless folk.' We always prepare supper in case wanderers like you come along. So far, if anyone parishes in this land, they become lost souls like us. The only hope of leaving this terrible place is if the one who holds the mighty mud pearl frees us. But how that works, no one yet knows."

"I have the mud pearl!" Heather blabbed.

Roused from their chairs, the headless folk tuned into her.

"You do?" shouted Bobby.

"Then you must secure it safely and fulfill your destiny. Don't let anyone else know about it. You probably shouldn't have told us that," said Percy.

"Sorry. I guess I should have known better," admitted Heather.

"Thank goodness, there is hope at last!" said Lilly.

Heather then took the opportunity to switch the topic. "Can I ask everyone a more personal question?" she asked.

"Certainly, dear," responded Sally.

"How come you all don't have heads?"

"Well," began Sally. "We were killed by the scarecrow a long time ago."

"How awful!" exclaimed Heather.

"Indeed. We were once friends of Farmer Hagglehoff back in your world, but got lost in the fields one day. And not too far along, the scarecrow decapitated us with his mischievous hand."

"Why?" Heather asked.

"We are not sure, but we now know that that scarecrow was once Farmer Hagglehoff."

"My goodness! You mean he turned evil?" said Heather.

"Yes," they responded in unison.

Heather decided this might be true. No wonder the scarecrow looked so human. The thought of witnessing his rotting flesh stuffed and stitched nearly made her lose her appetite.

"How did that happen to him?"

"We don't know," answered Sally. "The farmer was last seen reaping the fields aimlessly before he somehow became a mindless scarecrow. We tried to find the farmer one day, but instead *this* happened. In the morning, the scarecrow scares off crows from the post you saw early on as part of his curse, but then wanders about in the evening until dawn slaying the heads off his victims. Fear is all around."

"Why heads?" Heather asked.

"Nobody knows," responded Sally Breen.

A black spot of sorrow appeared on the left wing of Heather's ladybug pendant, representing the sorrowful fate of the headless folk and of the poor farmer. She quivered.

"Enough frightening stories for one night. Would you like us to sing you to bed, my child?" asked Lilly.

"Yes, please," responded Heather, feeling rather sleepy and hoping to not have nightmares. The four headless ghosts sang woebegone words that gave her hope:

We comely Headless Folk singing the night
Lost our heads from scarecrow hands in utter fright
Now stuck in his dreadful plan
Hoping someone will free the land
Hoo-lulu-hoo-lulu
Hoo-fee-doo-lalu
The Mighty Pearl she retrieves
Restores hope if she believes
The end not far but the darkness thick
The Land restored if she won't quit
hoo-lulu-hoo-lulu
hoo-fee-doo-lalu

Heather dozed into a pleasant sleep where she dreamed being with her loving students and family back home.

INTO THE MAGIC CORNFIELD

PART II
The Witch

CHAPTER

7

Heather awoke to a misty dawn, slouched in the chair beside the dying fire pit. Light beamed through the ugly forest canopy, making it easier to see, and the terrain in front of her looked more spread out than before. The Headless Folk were gone that morning, like most ghosts of lore. The only evidence of their presence was the campsite. Her shoes and socks lay beneath her, clean. In fact, she was clean herself. Hoping they could still hear her, she whispered thanks to them. However, it dawned on her that she would have to get her shoes in the mud again. But then she realized she could travel barefoot, since the ground was moist and soft. Tying her shoes to her shoulder sack, she left the sanctuary after eating a few more potatoes.

After a long trek, it was hard for her to sit down anywhere without getting her bottom wet.

Finally, she spotted a large rock. But a long neck craned out from under it and spooked her out of her seat. It wasn't a rock after all—it was a tortoise.

"Nice of you to stop by," he said.

"Pardon me," she replied, feeling terrible for sitting on the tortoise's shell that also had a red boutonnière.

"No trouble. Could you kindly bend those cornstalks toward me? My long neck still can't quite reach the ears." There were a few healthy, normal-size stalks behind him, which were not common in the area.

Heather did as he asked, and the reptile chomped one down to bits. He smiled and asked, "Do you need a ride on this hindering earth, ma'am?"

"That would sure make things easier on me," she replied. "Though, I always tell my students never to take rides from strangers. But you're a tortoise, so that makes it okay."

"Tordis is the name," said the tortoise as she saddled on top of him.

"Please to meet you, Tordis, my name is Heather."

"At your service, Heather."

However slow they rode, she at least had the chance to rest her feet.

"I have really come here to meet up with my lost partner, Poppy," said Tordis. "We were sold as tourist attractions to the old farm, and got tired of being pestered by little children all the time. We always dreamed of escaping into the fields and having everything to eat without any distractions. Poppy and I have a long history together, you see. We were shipped from place to place and fell deeply in love. But then we started fighting a lot. We fought and fought for a long time and even started biting each other, until one day she busted through the wooden gate and wandered into the cornfields without me. I attempted to follow her, but got lost. I was sad and angry, so I broke open the fence with my shell when the coast was clear. Now, here I am, looking for her."

"Oh, Tordis," said Heather. "You are very brave. But sometimes in life, we have to step back and ask ourselves, 'Are we really happy?'"

"We are happy!" he barked at her stubbornly. "Well, sort of, I guess…up until…"

"Now, now, Tordis." She tried to pacify him gently. "I don't want to tell you what to do, but sometimes in life it is best to let things go."

"I can't!" he sobbed in confession.

"Yes, you can," she assured him. "Not too long ago, I thought I was going to be in love with a man forever. But then we started fighting, too, before he hurt me. You don't want that in your life. We all make mistakes. But we all must strive to move on toward the light. Love isn't all about romance, you know. Love can be anything, anywhere. You can love your mother, father, child, neighbor, co-worker, pet, and many, many more. Love can be easy, and love can be hard. It can be simple, and it can be complex. That's why we are here on this earth: to love. Romance isn't everything. Remember that."

Tordis cleared up his tears. "Thank you, Heather, for your kind words of wisdom. I'll consider that," he conceded.

"Keep moving in life, and don't stop when things get rough," she continued. "When you love and respect from your heart, others will follow in turn."

"To be sure."

"Say, how come animals won't talk back home where I come from?" she shifted.

"We communicate in ways that humans can't understand."

"I see," replied Heather. "Do you know why this land looks so ugly now?"

"No. The ears don't taste all that great, either. I may not be that quick on my feet, but my shell protects me wherever I go."

"I wish I had one right now," she said.

Continuing to stroll through the dreary forest, she then decided it was time to disembark once the ground became firm. "You can stop over there, Tordis. I can walk again." She pointed to a giant weed-like cornstalk that was black as soot. He dropped her off in front of it.

"It was a pleasure meeting you, Heather. I think I'll stop looking for Poppy and just have her find me instead, if she wants to. In the meantime, I will seek out love and happiness in other ways."

"Good idea!" she said.

"Ta-ta." Tordis saluted her and roved away.

Heather studied the hideous stalk with snaky shoots and scimitar leaves, wondering if she could climb all the way to the top to see everything that stood before her. She hung her shoulder sack on a leaf and began to climb the tower, holding onto every branch she could find. Occasionally, she slipped and tore her clothing, which slowed her down, but she was determined not to fall. Her fear of heights was tucked away in the back of her mind and she refused to look down.

Finally, Heather climbed her way out of the canopy and into the emergent layer that briefly blinded her with light. A swarm of tall vegetation blanketed the earth across the horizon with soaring hawks from a distance; there seemed no end to this labyrinth. She moaned in disappointment and climbed back down to obscurity.

8

eather retrieved her shoulder sack and heard a loud thumping in the distance. While she stood there, curious to see what was causing the raucous, a giant squash with legs stomped its way into view, flattening the stalks and squelching the earth. The master center had the carved face of a jack-o-lantern and smiled sadistically at her.

"Beware, my lady, or you'll be *squashed* by the Giant Squash! Ha-ha!" the juggernaut blared in a creaky voice. The legs oscillated up and down in her direction.

"No way!" she exclaimed and dashed off.

Heather was alert as a hawk. But the beast's long strides quickly caught up with her. Quickly rethinking her course of action, she made an arc to stall the giant. But within moments, the squash pivoted and headed her way again. As the monster crept up to her, she ran in between the great legs. Her athletic prowess was owed to her days of basketball in school.

After a little cat-and-mouse, she managed to climb onto one of the squash's legs. Up and down she went, holding for dear life. Looking up, she realized the leg was attached to a sliding guide that ran inside a side slot bolted vertically onto the side of the squash's body. She looked to the back of the hull and found a huge wind-up key and gears. The squash was mechanical!

Heather grabbed ahold of the key and slowly revolved counterclockwise.

"Where are you, lady?" called the giant. The voice seemed metallic, and she reasoned that a microphone must have projected a speaker from inside the contraption.

Heather examined the gadgets thoroughly to see how she could sabotage the operation of the machine. It then struck her that she might be able to obstruct the gears somehow, forcing the inside spring of the key to lock up, shutting down the system. Glancing around her, she searched for a long ear to do the job.

In good time, the juggernaut stopped to scan the terrain, and she took the opportunity to snatch a sturdy brown cob, the length of her forearm, nearby.

"Come out wherever you are…I just want to *squash* you!" the squash monster blared. When it proceeded to stomp some more, the key guided her closer to the gears. Tiring from hanging arms, she at last shoved the ear between the rivet, forcing the machine to lock up. Heather let go of the key and landed on the ground. The inside gadgets made a big clamor that sounded like raining trash cans. Smoky flames billowed outward.

"Dah!" a small voice groaned after the commotion. The top lid from the master head opened out, and a cockroach the size of Heather's thumb crawled down to confront her on its hindlegs. A small top hat rested on its head, and a small tailcoat draped its back. The antennae were shaped in the form of whiskers.

"You ruined my machine! It took me years to build!" pouted the little insect with arms akimbo.

"Are you crazy?" Heather scolded him in righteous anger. "You could have killed someone!"

"Funny how you should mention that. I'm tired of big creatures like you trying to squash me all my life. Now it's time for me to try squashing back!"

"Well, maybe if you wouldn't trespass into other people's homes and eat their food, you wouldn't be squashed on so much," Heather said.

"You humans get all the good stuff, like sugars and cereals, while we pitifully scavenge the floors in desperation!"

"Do you know that cockroaches are known to carry diseases?" she countered.

"So does any other animal," returned the cockroach.

"Well, we won't take the risk!"

Heather picked him up by the hind legs to chastise him up close. "Not only should you learn not to trespass on others, but you should also learn not to take your anger out on innocent people." The cockroach bit her finger in retaliation, and she flicked him with her index finger yards away. "Be gone, you pipsqueak!"

The disgruntled bug turned around and futilely shouted back at her, "The scarecrow will get you for this! He'll complete what I failed to do!"

Heather called back to him, but he disappeared before she could advance.

She moved on with a second spot of sorrow on the left wing of her ladybug pendant due to the pitiful hatred from the cockroach.

Feeling a little chilly, she remembered the Silkworm and opened her shoulder sack. "Are you done with my silk coat now, Mr. Silkworm?" she asked him.

"Your coat is ready, Madam," he said. To her amazement, a beautiful white moth flew out of her bag to greet her kindly. "Wear it at your comfort. It is double-layered and beautiful."

Heather pulled out a gorgeous, chic white coat woven from the shoulders to the legs. It even had a hood. It was thick and shiny, perfect for warmth. She adored it covetously.

"This is perhaps the best gift I have received yet, Mr. Silk Moth. I honor your marvelous gift of Nature. Thank you."

"I appreciate your lovely words, my dear. I worked extra hard for you, since you have allowed me to complete my life cycle. Now that I no longer have to eat, I can go on to furnish my own offspring before I pass on. You have all my sincere regards to the completion of your journey. I must be off. Oh, and by the way, you have some extra silk in there in case you need any." A small mesh of silk was left in her bag. She thought it best to be used for darning stockings or mittens. "Adieu, Heather," he said.

"Adieu, Mr. Silk Moth." And that was the last she saw of him, for he flew on to fulfill his life in the air. A second spot was found on the right wing of her necklace due to her deep gratitude toward the silk moth. She put the cozy coat on and continued her track like an angel in darkness.

Heather tried to be extra careful in preserving the silk fabric, since it was bound to become a great souvenir.

A while later, the ground hardened. Small voices chanted in the background and Heather traced it to a long, circular enclosure of gray maize nearby. Smoke emitted from inside the center, and the voices became more distinct as she got closer. Putting her shoes back on, she asked herself, "What could be such a celebration?"

She crept into the plant enclosure on her knees and peeped through the other side that had an arena of cracked clay ground and a crowd of dancing people only two feet tall. They had dark skin and were partially clothed in corn cuttings. The race of these natives was unknown to her. They seemed to resemble Australian aborigines to her. The men held small stalks with pointy ears for spears. Three-foot domes made of mud and plants stood farther back. Earthen drums and flutes were mostly derived from maize. Men, women, and children gracefully danced around the great fire chanting:

> *We worship corn*
> *Since we were born*
> *Dancing in the maize*
> *For it is told*
> *The plant of gold*
> *Shines spirit night and day*

The ritual continued until a sounding horn called. The inhabitants sat in a circle around the fire, facing the foremost dome. Six warriors filed by the doorway as a small, elaborately clad man came out with pomp. Their chief had just entered. The constituents all sat in silence as he seated himself near the flames.

"Today, my people, we celebrate the gift from the Goddess of Gold, for she has left us her spirit in the golden plant," the chief said. "We pray that one day she will deliver us from the curse of our shortness. Now eat, my people. Our rare cobs are the most precious gift of our God. Orange, pepper, blueberry, grape, mint, meat flavor! Yes! And more!"

The warriors passed down bags of strange ears of different colors. The orange ones must have had an orange flavor, while the red ones must have had the peppery flavor; blue for blueberry, purple for grape, green for mint, and mahogany for meat. Everyone ate heartily, including the chief and his soldiers, until Heather failed to hold her nose from the spicy pepper corn and sneezed.

Alarmed, every little inhabitant stood up. "What was that?" demanded the chief. "Find the source!"

The armed men traced her sneeze and seized her with hoisted spears. She gasped once they caught her and tried to run away, but they encircled her. Then they brought her to the chief where everyone gasped at her height.

"Who are you, large lady? Why are you here?" asked the chief.

"I was only curious. I didn't mean to interrupt your feast. Let me go."

"Not so fast!" shouted the chief.

"Sire," whispered his assistant into his ear. "She could feed us all very well since she is made of meat."

"Hmm," pondered the chief. "Madam, meat is scarce around here and we get most of it from eating our dead. You, on the other hand, could feed our tribe for weeks. Therefore, I give the order to have you roasted!"

"You can't eat me!" shouted Heather. "I am a living soul!"

But the warriors rolled a barrel-size ear that knocked her backwards onto a net of rope they preset for her. They quickly tied her up and began dragging her to a rotisserie they started to assemble.

She shouted at them in rage, "You barbaric cannibals! Savages!"

How can I get out of this mess? she thought to herself. *I don't have anything sharp to cut with. What can I use to get them to stop?* Suddenly, an idea popped into her mind, *Maybe I could stay their actions if I entice them with the mud pearl.*

Though Heather wasn't supposed to reveal it to anyone, she figured she had to break this vow to save her life. Struggling to reach her sack with constrained arms, she managed to unzip the secret compartment.

Wielding the mud pearl to the sky, she shouted, "Behold, for I bear the mud pearl!"

The natives stopped, dropped their jaws, and widened their eyes over the artifact. The chief stood speechless.

"Release her!" he commanded.

The warriors untied her as everyone bowed down to her. She was surprised by the gesture.

Heather hastily stashed the mud pearl into the general opening of her shoulder sack with leftover silk.

"The Goddess of Gold has answered us! Forgive us, Goddess of Good, for blindly mistreating you. We all worship and repent for your Grace, for it is you we believe have been sent to deliver us from evil." The chief bowed.

Heather was curious and wondered, *Were these people persecuted?* She wanted to see their faces.

"Rise," she commanded. They stood up. "Who are you?"

"We're the Diminished Nixis," said the chief. "We were not always this small. In fact, we were almost as tall as you. You see, we find rare, flavored corn throughout this ghastly land to survive famine. The barren stalks you see around you weren't always this way, you know. Before an eroding flood, they used to be very graceful and elegant with many streamlets. We used to trade some of our rare cobs with a witch named Razzle Haring in exchange for her delicious gourds. But one day, a group of my servants ate her pumpkin pie behind her back while conducting business. When she found out, she became mad and gave them warts on their noses. After having to burn off the warts, we decided to trade some bad corn with her in retaliation. The witch then sought revenge by exchanging a magic gourd that shrunk us upon eating it. We've been this way ever since, hence the name, the Diminished Nixis. With our small stature, we especially live in fear of a mad scarecrow we scarcely avoid with fire; many of my people have been beheaded by him."

Heather saw the sadness in the tribal people's faces. Feeling sorry for their woes, a spot appeared on the left wing of her red necklace.

"We believe you, Goddess of Good, were sent to us by the Goddess of Gold, for it is told that whoever receives the mud pearl receives virtue. If you find the cure for our curse, we will make you our queen, and you can have all our delicious delicacies you wish."

Heather listened carefully to their plea. "I don't have any intentions of becoming queen, but I will do as you ask, only on one condition. No…two."

"What are they, Your Highness?"

"That you promise not to eat any more live people and stay out of trouble next time."

"You have our sincere word, your Grandness," assured the chief.

"Then what must I do?" asked Heather.

"Since we no longer do business with the witch, on account of her not letting us near her property anymore, you must approach her, acting oblivious to your connections with us. You will act as a new farmer who harvests the giant pepper corn she loves the most. But to do that, you must ask for the mysterious ingredient that causes them to enlarge. If she has the ingredient, offer to exchange giant pepper corn for it. We will give you a red ear just in case she asks for proof of your vocation. Oh, and one more thing, try to retrieve the magic gourd just in case we grow too tall upon your delivery, you never know."

"How do I get there?" inquired Heather.

The chief pointed to a fixed trail of sunflowers forking out of the enclosure, which curved left. "We made a trail that will take you directly to the witch's hut."

"Okay." Heather nodded. "I'll do it."

"Hurray!" They shouted in joy and danced a little upon handing her a red pepper cob. Then, they saluted her as she set out onto the trail.

CHAPTER
9

The pathway of sunflowers basked in light beams from the dark forest canopy. Their pleasantness made Heather smile. She kept smiling for no conscious reason at all, as if she were enchanted.

The involuntary gayness lifted as Heather exited the sunflower trail and then she stopped. *I could use some sunflower seeds on my way*, she thought. She turned back to the nearest sunflower head and began to pick out its seeds one by one, laying them in a depression she made in her silk coat.

When she turned away upon finishing, a loud voice boomed behind her, startling her into dropping the seedlings all over the cracked ground.

"Give me back my sunflower seeds!" it shouted. The robbed sunflower head tilted toward her in anger. "You stole my beautiful face. Now put them back in me!"

"I'm sorry, but I didn't realize you were conscious," she said.

"Well, you do now! So, put them back in me!"

His surly manner irked her. "If I take your face now, you will grow a fresher one later on," she reasoned with him.

"No! I like it just the way it was," the stubborn head said.

Heather thought the creature was very rude. "I didn't mean to trespass on you, sir, as I am used to picking seeds from unconscious sunflowers. But I have to get to the witch's hut and I just don't have time to replace your seeds, I'm sorry. But don't fret, my good sir, you'll grow a new face in due time." Heather smiled and proceeded to walk onward.

"Wait!" called the sunflower, and his ray flowers radiated like the sun. She unwittingly turned around and broadly smiled at the creature, as if she were forced to.

"You like smiling bright and sunny like a sunflower, eh?" it asked. "Well, if you don't restore my inflorescence at once, I'll change you into a smiling sunflower forever!"

The brightness waned, and Heather was herself again. "There are too many scattered among the cracks and crevices. It will be impractical finding them all," she protested.

"Well, I guess you'll have to try, then," sneered the sunflower.

Heather grumbled and searched on her hands and knees to gather what seeds she could find. It seemed she was there for a little less than an hour. Several times she placed some seeds back into the sockets, only for them to fall out. On a couple of occasions, she thought she had finished the job, only to be informed by the fickle sunflower head that few seeds remained.

Finally, the plant declared, "Ah…fresh as new."

She mumbled beneath her lips as she left with annoyed relief.

After the sunflower trail, old sign posts that said "Witch's Hut" pointed in the direction of the witch's home along a continuing trail of scrub. She made another left turn and saw a pig in a puddle with a pot belly.

He smiled at her with big, ruddy cheeks. "Hello there, little madam."

"Hello there, Sir Pig," she greeted.

"Don't mind me. I'm just taking my bath. How are you?" he asked.

"I'm fine. How are you?"

"Splendid. I've been wandering the fields today, which is why I'm so dirty. I enjoy eating leaves and roots so much."

"Well, I'm glad you're faring well, although too much of anything is not good, you know," she said.

"I know, I know," replied the pig. "Would you be so kind as to scratch my back?"

Heather looked around for a stick. "Certainly, just a moment."

"If you scratch me, I'll give you a kiss!" the pig said.

"That won't be necessary," she said. "Here, I'll scratch behind your ears."

The pig grunted in delight. "Thank you, little madam. Where did you come from?"

"Back home on earth, if this isn't part of earth already. I'm a teacher—"

"Oh!" interrupted the pig. "A teacher. How nice! Why did you become a teacher?"

"Because I love children," said Heather. "And I feel I could improve the world if I taught the right things to new people."

"Most certainly," said the pig. "I remember my mother. She taught us piglets how to forage and what to eat and what not to eat. Animals are teachers, too."

"Yes," Heather responded. "Teaching is anything—from survival, to arithmetic, to teaching about life and love."

"Well said," said the pig. "Every animal serves a good purpose. You humans are unique back on earth. You can think of things much more deeply and profoundly than other living things. There must be a special purpose to serve with that gift."

"I think so, too," said Heather. "Humans have a great responsibility to preserve, protect, and improve the world. Maybe even the universe. But I get very sad when humans do horrible things. It's like we are not doing what we are supposed to be doing."

"But you are a teacher," said the pig.

"Well, yes," Heather replied.

"So you like to learn and teach the right things. In that way, you are already preventing horrible things from happening."

Heather paused. "You're right," she realized. "We can all prevent them by our own free will."

"One can change many," added the pig.

"You obviously think like a smart human should, Sir Pig."

"I guess I surprise myself sometimes," he returned.

"You deserve a good back scratch." Heather gave him a nice posterior massage.

The pig grunted in delight again.

"Nice meeting you. Never stop learning," she said to him, ready to depart.

"Never stop teaching," returned the pig. "Be careful out there," he warned. "There's a lot more mud up ahead."

C H A P T E R

10

The bushy plants shielded the sunlight, and mist covered her path, thickening every step she made. The ground was slushy, making her totter side to side while barefoot.

Suddenly, Heather fell into a hole the length of a well and landed in a cool puddle. Her magic silk coat kept her clean. Stuck in nowhere, she attempted to climb out and call for help, but then heard light splashing directly below her.

Five tiny creatures leaped up from the watery pit. Their heads were like frogs' heads and their bodies were shaped like fish. The eyes were mounted side by side at the very top of their heads, and their mouths were agape. A dorsal fin in the shape of a shell was prominent, but the interesting part about them was the hopping of their pectoral fins.

"Hello there. Are you stuck?" one of them asked.

"Yeah, where am I?" she responded.

"You're in a magic mud hole. It moves around from place to place, from time to time. We live here because the moisture allows us to breathe. We are the Dancing Mudskippers; we dance through the mud with our fins."

"That's nice. But how can I get out of here?" she asked.

"Why, you must dance."

"What?"

"Dance! Dance like a mudskipper! Every time you dance correctly like us, the ground will lift higher till you reach the top."

"Dance in the mud?" she exclaimed.

"Well, yes. *We* do it. Try it!"

And with that, the mudskippers demonstrated their marvelous moves while she attempted to mimic them. It was hard enough to keep up with them in such a splashy confinement, but the bottom did lift each time she got it right. The mudskippers sang whimsical jitterbug tunes while they all danced in joy:

Dance like a mudskipper doo-wop-bop
Dance like a mudskipper to the pop
Dance to a mudskipper and don't you stop
Splishy, splashy till you drop
Dance to the mudskipper in the mud
Dance to the mudskipper not a dud
Dance like a mudskipper make no thud
Swishy, swashy and up you'll bud!

The dancing continued many times over until she finally reached the top.

"You did it! You danced like a mudskipper!" they cheered her.

"Thanks, you guys," she said back. "It was real fun. I just hope I don't have to do that again."

"Don't worry," said a mudskipper. "Just watch your step next time. And if you ever get stuck, remember, just dance like a mudskipper."

"Okay," she said and waved them goodbye. A third spot appeared on the right wing of her ladybug pendant from the joy of dancing with the mudskippers.

C H A P T E R

11

The dark ambiance lifted as the hideous plants became more spaced apart. It was almost sunny at the witch's locale, and the damp soil had moss and toadstool overgrowth. A field of pumpkins varied remarkably in size over the homestead—some normal, some humongous, and some as small as a mouse. The biggest pumpkin made a home for the witch. It had a door and a couple of windows with flowers. A small squash garden made up the backyard of the house. They too grew tremendously in size.

Maybe this is where the mad cockroach got his squash frame, Heather thought.

To the side of the house was a flowing brown river. The door of the pumpkin cottage opened and out came a frumpy old woman with galoshes and a gardening apron. She carried with her a watering can with a rose spout and began to sprinkle a glittery rainbow substance onto a small pumpkin nearby.

Within a few seconds, the pumpkin expanded about a foot in diameter.

"The magic formula!" Heather exclaimed to herself. She put her shoes back on.

While the witch fed another pumpkin, Heather approached the lady. "Excuse me, ma'am, but are you Razzle Haring?"

As the stooped witch turned to face her, Heather saw that the old crone's eyes were reptilian-like and had sharp pupils and yellowish sclera. The elderly woman had wrinkled grayish skin with a pointy, wart-ridden nose and small, serrated teeth when she smiled. Her fingernails were long and jagged. She didn't look very human, after all.

"Yes, I'm the witch, what can I do for you, my dear?" she spoke in a gentle yet strange manner. Heather's instincts told her something wasn't right about her.

"I'm here for business regarding your magic formula," Heather said.

"Step into my office," returned the witch. She set down her empty can and led Heather into the pumpkin cabin.

The hollowed interior was preserved in orange stucco and the floor was leveled with wood. It was a single room with a kitchen, dining table, and bed. Spiders were making her doilies. Shelves of various elixirs hung about. Lizards, snakes, amphibians, and a perched hawk also dwelled inside.

"Would you care for some of my delicious pumpkin pie?" The hoary witch pointed Heather to the rich dessert with a knife and plate in the middle of the table.

"Um, um, no thanks. I'm fine," Heather responded, distrusting the witch.

"Oh, all right! I'll take a piece first if that makes you feel any better," the old woman snapped, seeming to be slighted by Heather. She took a sliver of the pie, ate it, and opened her mouth. "See," she said. "Nothing happened to *me*!"

Heather took a slice for herself. The taste was delightfully sweet and creamy. No wonder the Nixis gobbled the whole dish behind her back in bad manners.

"So, state your business," Razzle said calmly, picking out one of her petite cherry pumpkins from a basket to snack on as a bitter delicacy. Their tiny size must have been from the work of the magic gourd.

"I'm trying to set up a giant pepper corn farm, but I need some of your magic ingredients to do the job," Heather explained.

"Oh, I just love pepper corn. I used to use it in many foods and even in some of my spells, but I haven't had any lately, not since my last suppliers burned bridges with me. It's funny, though, that I've never seen you before. You don't seem the type that would want to get dirty over harvesting such rare, oversized plants." The beldame suspected Heather. "Can you show me proof of your vocation?"

Heather paused to think about how to ward off suspicion and then remembered. "I can show you some of my red pepper corn." She hastily opened her shoulder sack to grab the ear entangled in silk threads. Inadvertently pulling out the two sticking items, the mud pearl got caught in between and landed on the floor. As it rolled, the witch's eyes widened in surprise.

"The mud pearl!" the old lady exclaimed. Heather swiftly grabbed the pearl and put it back safely into its secret compartment before handing over the cob.

The witch briefly glanced over the evidence before looking up at Heather in suspicion. "Are you telling me the truth about yourself?"

"Y-yes," Heather stuttered.

"Were you sent by the Diminished Nixis?" the witch asked.

"No," returned Heather.

"Hmm. Excuse me for a second." Razzle walked over to a black clay jar and opened its lid to reach inside. "Here's the secret ingredient!" The witch tossed a navy-blue ball to Heather, which erupted into a cloud of dark blue powder when she caught it.

Heather coughed. "Hey! What are you doing? What was that?"

The powder dissipated and small handprints glowed blue all over Heather's clothing.

"Aha!" Razzle pointed to the handprints. "You *were* sent by the Diminished Nixis, weren't you?"

Heather couldn't believe the guile of the old witch. She got nervous.

"Okay, you got me," she confessed. "But the Diminished Nixis mean you no harm. They're sorry for inconveniencing you. All they want is their height back. You'll never hear from them again."

"The Diminished Nixis are clumsy fools. They had a lot of nerve crossing me!" the hag said.

"But don't you think they've had enough punishment? I think you've triumphed long enough in your 'just' satisfaction. So please, give them back what is so precious to them."

Razzle stood while considering the argument. "What if I were to offer you the magic ingredient in exchange for the lovely pearl that just rolled out?"

Heather swiftly responded, "No, no. That's too precious for me to give away."

"Humph!" grunted the witch. Razzle then smiled wryly. "Well, all right. One pepper corn for one magic corn."

"Magic corn?" asked Heather.

"That's the secret ingredient. It's rare and grows wild in a secret garden I made a little way from here. You'll need a guide with you, so…ah! I've got it." After looking around her elixirs, she reached for a basket-sized jack-o-lantern with an eerie grin from her kitchen window and placed it on the table. The witch opened the pumpkin's lid and pricked her index finger with a needle to draw a drop of blood into the carved pumpkin. After chanting a few unknown words, Razzle handed the lifeless melon over to her.

"This will be your guide on your way to the magic corn."

"This?" Heather asked.

"Yes. Now go now."

Heather took the jack-o-lantern and headed out. The glowing handprints on her clothes had faded away. By the time the door closed, a mellow voice spoke below her.

"I am your guide, hon."

Heather flinched and noticed that the jack-o-lantern was talking to her, mouth in motion. "Golly," she muttered.

"There are three obstacles to overcome before seeking out your goal," the orange face told her. "Are you ready?"

"No..."

CHAPTER

12

They wandered through the pumpkin patch until they came upon a small onion field. The bulbs were big and fat, and they started to sneeze, which caused Heather's eyes to water and itch.

"Hmm…" said the jack-o-lantern. "It looks like Razzle's onions need water. If they don't get any after a certain time a day, they will sneeze irritants. Go get that can from the well over there and give them some water."

Heather found an old scrappy well with a rusty flowering can on top. She sprinkled down a few rows of onions, and they immediately stopped sneezing.

"That's much better," she said with relief.

Next was a mossy platform bordering a small cliff. Alongside the split hillock were two giant toadstools aligned according to height, from small to large. Lying next to the shortest one was a barrel-sized kettle gourd.

"This is your first obstacle, my lady," said the jack-o-lantern. "You must seat yourself on that gourd and bounce your way up the toadstools to the top of the cliff."

"Do you think I look like a child to you?" she asked.

"Of course you do," teased the pumpkin referring to her still-young baby face. She lifted her brow. "It's a bouncing kettle gourd. I'll show you how it works." The pumpkin leaped out of her hands and bounced on top of the first toadstool, which propelled him upward onto the next toadstool, which propelled him onto the moist hilltop. "That's how you do it," he called to her. "Try it."

Heather unwillingly made her way toward the outsized gourd. She positioned herself on the crown and held onto the long handle dipper, like a sit-bounce-ball. With little momentum, she immediately bounced. Practicing on the slippery flora, she fell off a few times.

Getting adjusted, she bounced on top of the first toadstool only to lose her balance and fall back onto the soft ground with no harm. Heather grumbled and tried again, this time being successful, but fell off the second toadstool. After the third try, she at last landed onto the moss-covered cliff-top alongside her guide.

"Well done, mademoiselle. Next comes the hard part."

"The hard part!" she griped. "Does Razzle have to do this all the time for someone her age?"

The pumpkin chuckled. "Maybe, maybe not," he returned.

"Umph!"

Proceeding with arrow signs, Heather came to a bizarre form of maize. Although this corn resumed a natural form, it flickered in red and orange and moved like fire, swaying uniformly in different directions. The leaf blades wavered, and the ears flared upward.

"This is the fire corn. You must wind your way through the twisty path within it," said the pumpkin. "These are necessary to guard her precious rarities."

Heather approached the brilliant corn and felt the heat. The plants probably couldn't be put out with water; in fact, they would probably grow with water. Studying the obstacle, she found the windy path within the brush. This was her only way through.

Heather tucked away her silk coat, entered the trail, and found the temperature to be tolerable, as long as she didn't stumble into the plants. Forced to zigzag her way through, the shifting stalks made her bend her body. Her clothes gathered a little smoke before she came to a break in the path.

The worst was yet to come, though. Blocking the exit way was a patch of small fire corn, about a foot tall, that stretched about three yards before terminating on common ground again. She only had a few yards of walking distance in front of her.

"Now, you must jump over that patch of small fire corn," the jack-o-lantern instructed.

"I don't like this!" she grunted.

"This is what you have to do, or your little quest would have all been for none," said the jack.

She took one deep breath, marched back to gather more momentum, and ran for a long bound. The back of her skirt lightly brushed onto the last plant, causing it to cinder a little, but luckily Heather made it unharmed.

"Mighty fine work," commented her little attendant. "The worst has passed, yet one obstacle still remains." Heather proceeded farther into the marked wilderness, respecting the moisture for once.

The final hurdle was a blockade of dark knotted corn.

"And now, for your last task," began the pumpkin. "Loosen the knotted corn in front of you to pass through. Be quick though, or it will knot up again. Are you ready?"

"But what if I get stuck and can't see in there!" she groused.

"Be quick and firm, and you may succeed. Be aware, though, this can get tiring."

Heather sighed and pried her way through the thicket as if arm wrestling in the dark. Occasionally, the lateral shoots in front of her reunited into knots after her arms fatigued. Paused in cluttered darkness, she cried out, "I'm tired and can't see a thing!"

"Perhaps you can put a shiny object inside me and use me as a lantern," suggested the jack.

"That might work," said Heather, and she took out the glowing mud pearl from her shoulder sack and placed it into the pumpkin. His face radiated to aid her sight.

"That's much better," said the guide, and she further pried her way through by jack-o-lantern light.

Finally, she squeezed her way through an open core that held a garden of unusual gourds and maize within a white picketed fence.

"You have reached your destination," announced the jack-o-lantern. Standing there in dazzlement, Heather looked at the most beautiful corn she ever saw; the kernels shifted in bright colors, and the gourds fluoresced as well.

"This is it! The magic corn and the magic gourd!" Heather declared excitedly. "What marvel..."

Setting down the jack-o-lantern, she opened the picket fence and picked a magic ear. Her face bathed in its mottled light. After placing it in her shoulder sack, she remembered the Nixis' request about the magic gourd. She picked the beautiful fruit from its emerald bearer and put it in. Lifting up her guide, Heather headed back out of the embankment with better ease.

As she paused to catch her breath on the other side, the pumpkin spoke again, but his voice shifted to a colder tone.

"Thanks for the mud pearl!"

Heather looked down to see a creepy grin that spat numerous leeches at her face. She ducked and screeched as three black, bdelloid tentacles emerged underneath the jack-o-lantern. The slimy, wriggly legs leaped from her arms while she struggled to ward off the attacking leeches. The legged jack-o-lantern disappeared into a murky stream nearby. The leeches meanwhile swarmed Heather's torso, relentlessly latching onto flesh. Desperately pulling them off, some of them managed to crawl back to her with front and rear suckers. She ran, tearing the bloodthirsty creatures off her skin until all were dispelled. Inflicted with minor suction wounds, she paused, staring at the dirty river and uttered in despair, "The mud pearl!"

13

Making her way back to the pumpkin patch, Heather marched up to the witch's hutch and barged through the door in anger. It was eerily empty though.

"Razzle! Where are you, you thieving harridan!" she shouted, but received no answer. Heather scanned every nook and cranny only to exit in frustration.

Facing the murky waterway, a large shadow overcame her. Behind the house appeared a dreadful toad the size of a rhinoceros with keen reptile eyes like Razzle's, defined teeth with extended canines, and black claws in place of lax toad fingers. It gave a sadistic grin fraught with warts.

"Heh, heh, heh," laughed the witch in her new form. "Did you like my trick? All it takes is one drop of blood and then you have a leech."

"You deceived me!" Heather cried out in righteous anger.

"Did you really think I was going to offer you the magic corn out of mere sympathy for the

Diminished Nixis? The only reason I did it was to steal the mud pearl. Its magic is abounding, and I can harness it all to my own discretion. Now, stay out of my way unless you want to be lunch!" The toad chomped at the air as a threatening gesture and began to walk off.

"Where are you going?!" Heather called to the fiend.

"I have a giant leech to catch. So long!"

"Witch!" returned Heather.

The giant crank sauntered off in pursuit of the artifact, leaving her hopeless by the river.

Heather approached the shore and sat on a rock in gloom, feeling a failure. Now the mud pearl was bound for wicked hands, and perhaps the land would never be restored to harmony again.

"This was a bad idea coming to the witch's hut," she thought to herself. "I should have never been so gullible as to hand over the pearl like that." Now her necklace had four black spots of sorrow on its left wing. Gazing somberly at the water, a lurking figure caught her eye from below its surface.

"Lempet!" she exclaimed.

"There isn't much time, Heather," he spoke gravely to her, gulping air. "A giant leech has the mud pearl and the witch is on her way to consume it. Luckily, she is headed in the wrong direction, for I know where the leech is. We must retrieve the pearl before she does."

"But how?" she asked anxiously.

"Go to the witch's hut and take a long fishing pole, a long hook, and a knife."

Heather went back into the pumpkin house without fuss. She deduced fishing out the leech was the logical solution. Looking about the cabin, she soon came across the items as large as sea tackle.

"I wonder what I am to use for bait?" she asked herself.

The witch's black rain boots were lying beside a wooden chair, and Heather put them on to allow her to move more easily in the mud and water. The witch's vinyl apron hung on a lumpy coat hanger of wood, and the brown gardening gloves rested on top of the table. Heather adorned herself with the accessories, tying her red handkerchief around her forehead. She walked out, determined, and said, "I have the equipment. What are we to catch the leech with?"

"Let's go," Lempet said without answering her question, and they traveled up the river in the opposite direction to where the witch was headed.

They moved through the miserable terrain until the grungy jack-o-lantern was spotted marooned onto shore. Heather picked up the hornswoggling jack and quickly noticed it was completely hollow and devoid of any life. Smashing it to the ground, she continued.

Eventually, they confronted a stagnant pond benighted with pond scum. Straggly weeds surrounded them, and the qualms of silence told a dire omen.

"The giant leech lays in that pond up yonder, Heather," Lempet announced.

"What do we do now?" she asked.

"I want you to hook me."

"Excuse me!" she said. "And use you as bait! Come now, there must be some other way around this."

"There is no time, Heather. The leech craves lots of blood. You will hook me and draw a drop of blood from my back with the knife to lure him to me. Since I am a lungfish, my blood will fill him up with air. The monster will become easy to reel in as his body will expand. Once you get ahold of him, slay the leech open with the knife to regain the mud pearl."

"But Lempet, this is a very risky job for you!" she protested.

"Heather, you must do this, or the fate of our world will forever be left in the hands of the witch. You are very strong and brave, but here lies a critical moment and we must succeed at all costs."

Heather reluctantly did what she was told. After carefully hooking Lempet by the mouth, she gently pierced his back with the knife with little pain. Gathering courage and strength, she headed up to the pond.

"Give me plenty of slack when he latches onto me," Lempet said. "Don't start reeling until he is blown up like a balloon. I'll tell you when."

She released Lempet into the shallows after his final request. From there, the lungfish swam toward the deep end and immersed himself, carrying the slackened line with him as a faint trail of blood followed behind.

Standing by the shore in brief silence, a tremendous tug from the fishing line jerked her forward. Ripples violently beamed across the turbid water as the beast took Lempet as its prey. Line rapidly flew out of the bale before a massive body breached the water's surface in a maddening rage.

A giant leech roared resonantly like a dinosaur with Lempet's caudal dangling from its horrendous mouth. The black goliath was the size of a professional wrestler! Yellow hooks spiraled down its reddish sucker, easily conceived of engulfing a human head. Red spots streaked down the segmented back. It was ferocious.

Heather briefly stood in awe as the sanguinary creature expanded from air, until Lempet's voice called, "Reel us in, Heather!"

The bale locked as she arduously reeled and tugged both the monster and the lungfish onto shore. Back and forth, she pulled hard and the leech resisted like a tug-of-war. But it would have been much more difficult hadn't the leech been buoyed with air.

When Heather seized the opportunity to lock the beast's head in her arms by the splashy water's edge, the leech suddenly spat the lungfish out and leeched onto her neck, sucking her lifeblood. Heather screamed in terror. She could feel pressure from the hooks but there was little pain, since the leech secreted a local anesthetic upon feeding. The sound of her blood gurgling out of her neck was evident, though, and she began to feel weary by the sudden exsanguination. She knew she had to act quickly or die from anemic shock!

Heather eyed the knife lying close on shore and forced her way toward it. The creature's bloated skin thinned like a balloon, and the texture was translucent enough to see the mud pearl glowing in the leech's innards.

Finally, after struggling for steps, she got close enough to grab the knife and jammed it into the leech's belly. The monster roared as gallons of blood burst out of the gash. The blood wasn't only the creature's. Heather, drenched in red, saw the glowing mud pearl slowly roll out of the beast. It soon gushed out into her hand as the leech monster collapsed back into the water to meet its grave. With a big gouge around her neck, she triumphed, possessing the beautiful mud pearl once again.

"We did it, Lempet!" she said.

The fish moaned from the shoreline.

Rushing to his aid, Heather saw that he was weak and limp. "Oh no!"

"I lost too much blood, Heather," the lungfish said in a fading voice.

"Lempet, you can't... No, please don't..."

"I'm sorry, Heather. I had a feeling this would happen."

"We should have used a different method," she said mournfully.

"It all ends here for me, my dear. Don't blame yourself," the dying lungfish said.

"Lempet!"

"I have served the mud pearl long enough to see it kept safe," he continued. "I had to do this so you could go on, Heather. Bring that pearl to victory, my heroine. You did well. I…"

Her throat tightened as she sobbed. "Lempet…" she moaned once more before he passed away.

The fifth spot of sorrow emerged from her necklace while Lempet slowly transformed back into a golden carp for the last time, but never opened his eyes again.

CHAPTER

14

After sitting by the banks for a long while in mournful respect, she gathered herself by suiting up into her silk coat before a large shadow overcame her. The giant, fanged toad stood over her again.

"I see you have reclaimed the mud pearl, eh? And in a very dramatic fashion," said the ugly witch. "Well, I'll spare your life if you toss it into my mouth and leave my lair forever. What do you say?"

"Never!" Heather exclaimed in fury, holding the pearl tightly in her fist.

A long, forked tongue like that of a snake flung out of the toad's mouth and latched onto Heather's wrist. "Then I shall eat you up with it."

The gaping witch reeled in her tongue. Heather reached for her shoulder sack with her free hand to grab the magic gourd. Once she got closer to the toad's nasty mouth, she hurled it down its throat.

Released, the witch coughed and shrank down to a normal, harmless little toad. "You brute! How dare you shrink me!" shouted the diminutive witch.

Heather picked up the amphibian by its hind legs and dangled it in front of her face for reproach. "Looks like you got a dose of your own medicine, Razzle. Now you know how the Diminished Nixis feel!"

Heather put the witch toad in a small wooden cage from the pumpkin house, then buried Lempet near the brown river with a cross and prayer. She washed and dried her clothes near a hearth, ate some spinach the witch had to replenish some of the lost iron in her blood, finished off the pumpkin pie, and took a long nap. Afterward, she discarded her old shoes and took the witch's dark brown moccasins and mud boots. Sequestering the cage in her shoulder sack, she went on her way back to the Diminished Nixis to hand over both the magic ingredient and their former conqueror.

CHAPTER

15

On the road at sundown, her neck wound throbbed painfully as the leech's natural anesthetic wore off. She remembered the extra silk the silk moth gave her and took it out to bandage her gouge. The pain and wound were remarkably gone within a matter of seconds, thanks to the silk's magical healing. Heather once again gave thanks for the magic silk moth, and further applied it to her other sores.

When she was done, Mr. Cob emerged with a gray face from an obscure stalk. "I'm sorry for what happened to Lempet," he said.

"Oh, Mr. Cob, it's so nice of you to see me again after I've been so blue," she replied. "Everything is wrong here. I want to go back home! Why is it so dark here?"

"We are in trouble, Heather. Just look at my face." Forlorn was obvious in him as he showed a gray frown. "Those who risk their lives to restore peace are

148

greatly honored by us, Ms. Hazelkind. We all share your mourning for the brave lungfish. The golden spirits speak to us all. You just listen for that golden spirit inside you. Put your heart and soul together and it will guide you wherever you go, in all hardships. Be brave and bring that pearl to victory."

Heather felt like crying.

"We are all in it together, Ms. Hazelkind. The golden spirits are with you." He disappeared again.

She strolled on, dejected, but then heard shuffling from the foliage behind her. Her hair follicles stood on end, her pupils dilated to their maximum size, and her heart drummed against her chest when she saw the mad scarecrow stomp his way toward her with his morbid sickle. Her feet felt like bricks as she stood there, frozen from the horrible sight of him.

"I want your head!" he growled and swung his weapon at her neck.

Heather ducked in time and fled, screaming down the path with the scarecrow in pursuit. "Leave me alone!" she yelled.

The mud boots she took from the witch helped her move faster, and the scarecrow gradually fell behind.

The stuffed fiend roared, wildly swinging his sickle until she reached the sunflower trail again. By then, the Nixis' campfire was in sight and the scarecrow fell back and disappeared into the ugly maize.

"Hurray!" the Diminished Nixis shouted as she barged her way through. She brightened a bit, but quickly looked back to see if the scarecrow was still present. He wasn't. All the Nixis crowded around her in praise as she presented them with the magic corn and the captive witch. A tribesman laughed at the imprisoned toad. Heather was crowned with a wreath of maize as their heroine.

They held a big feast following her arrival. Heather sampled all their delicious flavors with a stew of potatoes, cabbages, and beans.

The Diminished Nixis used a separate cauldron to strip the magic kernels in. The boiling water dispersed all the ingredients, and every Diminished Nixi drank a bowlful of the soup. One by one, they grew upward, though they turned out to be naturally shorter than Heather, on the order of pygmies.

Celebrating in glee, they then bowed down to her. "We thank you greatly, Goddess of Good, for you have fulfilled our prophecy of being tall again. As of now, we are no longer called the Diminished Nixis, but just Nixis," said the chief.

Every tribesperson jumped in joy and started dancing their best tribal rituals to their native music. Heather's necklace revealed the fourth spot of joy on the right wing. Once the celebrations wound down, everyone slept near the fire while some sentinels looked out for the scarecrow.

16

That night, the forest was pitch-black, except for the campfire. Silence dominated, except for the flickering flames. The guards fell asleep at their posts, and it must have been around midnight when a gentle clicking sound slowly awoke Heather from her deep sleep. Goosebumps started to arise from her skin as she thought of the scarecrow. But then a harmless cricket gently whispered to her.

"Don't fear, Heather, you have a message."

"What message?" she whispered back, taking care not to disturb the slumbering natives.

"Not sure. Please come with me."

"But what about the scarecrow?" she quietly asked him.

"He is not around. My wife, Shara, knows. She is in the air right now. Come, let us show you the way. You'll be back before you know it." Heather carefully stood up from her sleeping mat, laid her coarse blanket aside with little noise and followed the hopping critter into the dark maize forest. No one noticed her as she left. The cricket stopped to click a little tune into the sky.

"I click to stay warm, I click to communicate, Click is the name," he told her. The hidden moonlight was then replaced with chartreuse twinkling that weaved through the misty air. "There she is," said Click.

After more call-and-response communication, a large firefly made its way down to them. "Hello, Click," she quietly said to her mate.

"Hello, Shara, my light," returned Click. An odd, happy couple they were. "Are we here?"

"Yes. Ms. Hazelkind, you can use me as a lamp." The firefly landed on Heather's left index finger. "Ahead is how we communicate long distance in Maizeland, but the scarecrow destroyed most of these. Every person who participates has their own version of these plants. Messages can be sent back and forth between them when writing on the leaves. You have a few unread messages."

Heather approached a stout, dark green cornstalk with wide leaves. Stooping down while holding the firefly up for light, she grabbed a leaf blade with her free hand and held it close to the bug's glowing abdomen. The leaf fluoresced words of the same color as the firefly. It read:

153

> To: Heather
> From: Margaret Dune
>
> Heather, the bees are all gone.
> I sense doom coming, as I am
> feeling sadder by the day. You are
> our only hope. I wish I could be
> there with you, but I'm too old.
> Please restore our land with the
> mud pearl.

Heather felt pity over her old friend that she left behind. She wanted to see Margaret again soon.

"You can respond on the back with the leaf quill," said Shara, directing her to a slender shoot. Heather pulled the leaf shoot from the branch node and it revealed a pen tip. Using her firefly lantern, she turned the leaf message over and wrote in glowing ink:

> To: Margaret Dune
> From: Heather
>
> Mrs. Dune, stay strong and don't
> fret. The harmony of Maizeland
> will be restored, and the bees will
> return.

"You have two more messages," announced the lady fly. Heather reached for another leaf and read:

To: Heather
From: Sally Breen

Heather, I hope you're still around. Attached is a map for crossing the maize ahead. This can save you time. Beware the scarecrow.

Heather found a traced-out maze puzzle on the back of the leaf and tore it off. She then wrote on a blank note:

> To: Sally Breen
> From: Heather
>
> Sally, thanks for the directions. I will make it out okay.

Heather reached for the third letter and it shocked her to read:

> To: Heather
> From: Farmer Hagglehoff
> Heather, please help me!

PART III
The Scarecrow

CHAPTER

17

I n the early, misty morning, Heather awoke from a long sleep by the dying campfire, still unnerved by what she had read in the last message she'd received. She thought to herself, *Is the farmer still alive? Was it really him communicating with me? If so, how could he write me a letter while inside the scarecrow?* Heather hadn't responded to his message because she didn't know what to say or think. It was all too disturbing for her as it made her cringe. The thought of the poor farmer trapped in the scarecrow reminded her of the iron maiden used in medieval times where a prisoner, sometimes innocent, was tortured inside an iron cabinet covered with spikes and couldn't get out.

The cricket and his wife had left her to sleep after reading the messages the previous night, for they were nocturnal and couldn't accompany her in daylight hours.

A nice, warm bowl of mush was served to her for breakfast, and she took it gratefully. After, Heather said goodbye to all her native companions, for she had to reach the end of her quest and couldn't stay any longer. The Nixis escorted her out onto a dying trail that headed north and merrily waved goodbye. She waved back with her crown and bouquet.

For hours, she traveled on foot across the flood-ridden terra with no one around. Her new boots helped her move faster than without them, and her silk hood kept her head warm. At one point it began to rain, and she shielded herself with a broad leaf.

The climate gradually warmed and the ground hardened to crust. A grove with a small bed of large rocks with ancient paintings on them stood her way. Thorny vines smothered the ruins. There was even a bramble of blackberries nearby. She picked some to feast on and then spotted an interesting rock with a painting of a large pixie queen elaborately robed, overlooking a beautiful field, with smaller pixies kneeling around her.

Could this be the Goddess of Gold the Nixis told me of? she wondered. Small stone-carved seats stood everywhere in different sizes, possibly representing a hierarchy. Cherubic statues were corroded from the rain as a relic of a forgotten past. Heather saw another rock with a painting of tiny pixies laying a shiny pearl inside a clamshell.

The mud pearl? she thought, but couldn't make much sense of it.

Noon approached as Heather wandered further away from the bedrock area, and the air grew very humid and sticky. She removed her silk coat, but mosquitoes feasted on her. Slapping the bugs off, she shouted, "I can't stand these vermin mosquitoes!"

An abandoned carriage lay stuck in the dry mud ahead of her. Heather approached the stranded wreck and opened her way in.

"Ahem." uttered a turkey resting on a hay nest with eggs on the other side of the long passenger seat.

"Oh! I didn't know someone else was in here," said Heather.

"That's all right. You don't look threatening to me. You can sit down," the mother bird replied. Heather sat down alongside the turkey and closed the door.

The interior was worn with age. The seat coverings were tattered from the sun, the carpet was dirty, the walls were cracked, and the windows were grimy.

"What are you doing here?" the hen asked.

"I just had to get away from those pesky mosquitoes for a while."

"Don't worry, they come and go," the turkey assured her.

"That's good. What are *you* doing here?" asked Heather curiously.

"I escaped the farm from the other world because I wanted my chicks to grow up and fly like wild turkeys, instead of being fattened in cages for slaughter. My husband didn't bother to come since he was fat and lazy and said it was our lot in life, just like the other mindless birds, so I flew the coop."

"Oh!" said Heather.

The mother bird continued, "It isn't much of a haven here, though, since a mad scarecrow is on the loose."

Just then, the wind picked up outside the car as leaves rustled in the background. Heather looked out the unclean car window and saw a dust cloud approaching.

"Uh oh!" exclaimed the turkey. "Quick! Tie something around your face."

Heather quickly reached into her bag and pulled out her lucky handkerchief, then tied it around her nose and mouth.

"Hang on tight; we are going for a little ride," the bird told her.

"What do you mean? What about you?" Heather asked her.

"Don't worry about me. I've been through this before. Just hang on. We'll be all right."

The turkey buried her head in her feathers. Heather used both hands to grab hold of a leather handle bolted onto the ceiling of the carriage. She looked outside the window and saw the dust cloud getting closer. The violent debris nudged the vehicle once it consumed their space. The outside was brown, and Heather closed her eyes once dust seeped into the car.

Heather briefly opened her eyes when she felt the car being lifted up but had to quickly shut them from all the dust inside. They sailed through the air like a hot air balloon. The cab did not collide head-on with any of the large cornstalks outside, though it sometimes scraped along the leaves and branches. They must have been riding along the very edge of the current boundary layer to avoid a front impact. The carriage zigzagged through the forest by dust wind for several minutes until the brown cloud lost its strength. By then, it carefully lowered the vehicle onto the ground again and subsided.

Heather looked out the dusty window and the scenery looked about the same as before from her angle. She opened the door to vent out the remaining dust inside the coach then closed it to prevent the dust from drifting back in until it was completely gone.

"What was *that*?" she asked.

"That was the ghost of the Great American Dust Bowl," answered the turkey. "The storm comes to haunt us from time to time, and it nicely carries anything away with it."

"I know about the Dust Bowl," said Heather.

"You do?" questioned the turkey.

"Yes. I'm a teacher. The Dust Bowl took place in the Great Plains of the 1930s. Before the arrival of farmers, the prairies held the soil in place. But since the settlers plowed it all away, they disrupted the soil, causing it to blow up by the wind."

The hen butted in to add to Heather's lecture. "And a drought and economic depression also made matters worse. Millions of families abandoned their homes. Since then, a great deal has been learned about proper soil tillage."

"You are quite smart for a turkey," said Heather.

"Just because I am a hen doesn't mean I have to act like my head is cut off. No disrespect to the scarecrow's victims."

"Where did you get that knowledge?" asked Heather.

"This car came with an old history book."

"Wow," added Heather.

The turkey then lowered her voice as she shifted to a less enlightened tone. "You know, I don't think this land has been well taken care of since Farmer Hagglehoff died. It's so ugly, like the scarecrow."

"I know," agreed Heather. A long silence settled between them until Heather spoke up. "Anyways, I must be on my way. Thanks for sharing history with me, Mrs. Hen. I'm glad you found a safe place for your chicks."

"Watch out for the scarecrow!" informed the turkey.

"I will!" Heather stepped out of the carriage and patted herself down. The mosquitoes were gone. As she turned to the back of the coach, daylight temporarily blinded her and then it became clear that the eldritch forest she had wandered through for a long time had at last ended. The dust storm transferred her out.

There was a hay-pasture with bales about fifty yards ahead, which bordered another field of green verdure, like she remembered once. The sapphire sky was bluer than ever.

"All right!" she exclaimed. Throwing off her mud boots, Heather headed out of the darkness and into the light.

CHAPTER
18

The haystacks buckled upward like moving lips and sang bluesy tunes in acapella as she made her way through the pasture.

"That's very kind of you," Heather said to them. She then approached an entrance arch made of hay bales that ushered in a corn maze. A dented signpost read "Start Here" in front of the starting trail.

Heather took out the leaf message sent by the headless folk with the map and entered, following the pattern as best as she could. A few times she reached a dead end and retraced her path after realizing she had made a mistake.

A wooden bench stood in the middle of a widened area with three juniper trees a short distance behind it. She thought it would be a good time for a rest and sat down, then rubbed her feet as she watched a few ground squirrels scurrying about.

One of them quietly called out to her. "Psst! Below you. Take them!"

Heather looked below the garden bench and spotted what appeared to be carrot sprouts in the dark soil. She pulled them out from the earth.

"Thank you," she said, but the squirrels had already disappeared into the wall of cornstalks without reply. Heather ate a few carrots and saved the rest in her shoulder sack. Then she sat there for a little while longer, enjoying the gentle breeze and mild climate of the afternoon.

A hideous chorus of laughter startled her off her seat. Three jackrabbits the size of wolves stood by the juniper trees. They had warped muscles and visible rib cages. Their grizzly hair was coarse and unkempt with bald spots. The ears stood straight up with webs of veins running through them. Their long feet had elongated nails. Sharp-edged bucked-teeth were clearly seen from their strange grins, and their eyes were yellowish-pink with small, dark pupils.

"Pardon us, fair lady. I'm Long-Feet-Leary," spoke the rabbit with the longest feet.

"I'm Long-Eared-Eary," spoke the rabbit with the longest ears.

"And I'm Long-Teeth-Terry," said the last one with the longest teeth. The jacks all had a funny, high-pitched voice.

"Our master doesn't want anybody wandering through here. You have to leave now," said Leary.

But Heather was insistent. "I must get through."

"State your business!" snapped Leary.

"I need to get to the end of Maizeland," she replied.

"Ha-ha. As I said, Master doesn't want anyone to pass!"

"Who is your master?" she asked.

"The scarecrow," returned Leary.

Heather paused as a chill went through her, though she was still determined. She tried walking around the jacks to the next entrance but the rabbits blocked her off.

"Let me through!" she growled at them.

"We can tear you open," warned Leary.

"Stay back, you lugs!" Heather barked at them.

"Hmm...I bet she tastes sweet, too," Terry told the other jacks, licking his teeth. The three imps advanced toward her.

Heather saw a strange, colored coil beneath them and recognized the face of a serpent looking up at her, smiling. It was the milk snake she had met earlier, who had spared her from the crows.

"Look! Snake!" she yelled, pointing at him.

The jacks flung themselves up into the air in hysteria and collided with one another as the milk snake vanished. Heather ran onto the next trail that forked off in multiple directions. She chose one forking path and then ran off into another branching path.

Where did she go!" the jackrabbits exclaimed.

"You go that way, you go that way, and I'll go this way," the leader instructed.

To find her, Long-Eared-Eary used his long ears to hear Heather's footsteps. Long-Feet-Leary used his long feet to leap up into the air to see the maze ahead of him, and Long-Teeth-Terry chewed his way through the corn walls with his long teeth.

Heather further tried to lose the gang of three by wandering into different paths for about a minute but came upon a dead end.

"I found her!" Long-Teeth-Terry called out to his members after peeping through a wall from a distance.

A wave of adrenaline coursed through her body as she paced back and forth and side to side to find a way out. The jackrabbits joined up and proceeded to close in on her.

"It's suppertime, fellas!" Leary said to his pack.

"I really don't like meat," whispered Eary.

"Shut up! You do," Leary said. "We can do this the easy way or the hard way, lady," he hollered at her.

Heather backed up all the way against the thick wall of stalks when a strange ball of scales rolled into view and knocked the rabid jacks off their feet like bowling pins.

"That is no way to treat a lady!"

A courageous armadillo half her size stood in front of her with long, hooked claws and shiny armor plates. His body resembled a knight with cuirass, helmet, and gauntlets.

"I'll protect you, ma'am. The Armadillo Knight is here!" he declared, eyeing his enemies.

Gathering their senses, the three jacks got off the ground, and Leary said harshly to him, "Curse you, knight! Your strength is no match for our powers. Armis-muta-insoli-hexa!"

Eary wiggled his long ears, Leary stomped his long feet, and Terry chattered his long teeth. With that, the armadillo knight transformed into a soft-bellied opossum. Heather gasped.

"That's somewhat better," declared Leary, and the three hares continued to advance.

"Great Scott!" exclaimed the former armadillo, realizing his armor was gone. "But they won't get to us without a fight!" He bravely positioned himself right in front of her.

At that moment, Heather remembered the carrots she received from the squirrels and took them out, hoping to distract the hares' appetite as a last-ditch effort. She waved them in the air, and the hares shrank back and hid around a corner.

"Nice work!" commended the opossum.

"What's the matter? Don't you like carrots?" Heather taunted them.

"Carrots!" Leary exclaimed. "Heavens no! We're allergic to them!"

"We are?" Eary questioned him.

"Yes! Now shut up!" Leary snapped.

Taking a large bite to mock them, Heather said, "I'll tell you what. If you three promise to leave us alone, we won't poison you to death."

"Consider it done!" shouted the leader, and the three lagomorphs loped in a flash.

"Begone, you foul creatures!" the opossum hollered at them.

"Thank you for saving me, sir," she said to the heroic knight.

"No problem, madam. It is my duty to serve and protect the innocent. It was a good thing you had those carrots with you, otherwise we would have had more of a struggle on our hands. We all should carry protection with us somehow. You're very brave coming out here alone, you know. Let me escort you."

"Thank you, sir," Heather said. "But how do we transform you back?"

"Good question. I don't know. Hopefully, this spell isn't permanent," answered the opossum.

Heather paused, thinking of the mud pearl. Perhaps that might undo the spell.

"I've got something that might help you," she said, opening her shoulder sack. Heather took the pearl and concealed it in her hand.

"Look ahead," she told him. The opossum looked forward, not seeing what Heather had in hand and she touched the back of his head with the pearl.

He instantly turned back into a shiny armadillo knight.

"That was remarkable!" he exclaimed. "How did you do that?"

"I'll tell you in a little while," she replied, slipping the pearl back in her sack. She wanted to get better acquainted with the knight before telling him her precious secret.

"Do you know those punks?" Heather asked.

"Everyone knows those bullies. They are guardians of the scarecrow, a cowardly bunch," answered the knight.

"Why are they allergic to carrots?"

"They say they are, but I don't think it's true," he answered. "I just think it reminds them of being ordinary rabbits. And they dread being ordinary rabbits for whatever reason. The scarecrow taught them magic, you know."

Heather quietly gasped. *The scarecrow knows magic?* she thought in dismay. "Is he close by?" she asked.

"Possibly, but he usually roams around at night, and it isn't quite dusk yet."

"Are we close to the end of Maizeland?" Heather eagerly inquired.

"Everyone who crosses the corn maze is close to the end," affirmed the knight.

"Hurray!" she cheered.

"I wouldn't get too excited, though. Danger still lurks out there," warned the knight. "Do you know your way out of this maze?"

"Somewhat. I have this map with me," replied Heather, showing him the leaf.

"No need for that anymore. I've been through here many times and know the rest of the way."

"Oh, thank you!" she said.

The armadillo led Heather with ease as they got to know each other. The fifth spot of joy appeared on her pendant's right wing due to the knight's gallant chivalry.

"This world used to be protected by the farmer's loving magic, and armadillos were his soldiers," said the knight. "But now that he has turned into the scarecrow, this land may never be what it once was. It has been neglected for many years and has been ravaged with droughts, floods, plagues, foes, and so on."

"Have you heard of the legend of the mud pearl?" she asked.

"Yes, it is said to have the power to restore our land. Maybe it could also vanquish the scarecrow. The Wise Owl might know what to do with it."

"Who's the Wise Owl?"

"He resides just before the exit point, which is straight ahead after coming out of this maze. He is very wise as he has been around through the ages."

Heather decided to reveal her secret to him. "Do you know you were transformed back with the mud pearl?"

"You have the mud pearl!" exclaimed the armadillo knight.

Heather put her finger to her lips and whispered, "Shh."

"Of course." The armadillo promised to keep her secret hidden. "To be sure, I will accompany you all the way to the Wise Owl."

"Oh, thank you," Heather said.

As the late afternoon approached, they came to a sign that signaled the end of the maze. The next field ahead was being devoured by swarms of large, greedy grasshoppers that became so heavy from eating they could hardly fly. They looked like flying bowling balls. Other armadillos fought them back by launching into the air like cannons, swiping their gobbling opponents with their claws. Yet they were hopelessly outnumbered.

"Uh-oh!" uttered the knight, positioning himself in front of Heather. "Ms. Hazelkind, if by any chance we get separated in the fray, don't bother to find me. Just quickly continue straight ahead. I'll try to catch up with you."

They carefully crossed into the melee. The armadillo knight briefly engaged with some grasshoppers in front of him and stood his ground, but then one angry grasshopper swooped down and knocked him out of Heather's sight. Heather called to him but received no answer. Finally, she faintly heard his voice call in the distance, "Go on, Heather! Go on!"

She ran stealthily forward, shielding her face. Some of the grasshoppers bumped into her on the way. Before long, she was out of range of the battlefield with just herself, but the land was barren from being eaten up.

CHAPTER

19

The day ended as twilight bleached the sky like orange dye. The cool air made her don her silk coat as she walked down a trail. Not a voice was heard. The corn alongside her that wasn't consumed by grasshoppers looked sallow and had black blotches on them. Their shoots sagged over and wilted from disease. She could hear coughs echoing all around, but there wasn't a soul to see.

Chimney smoke billowed upward from down the vista, and she wondered if this meant the end of her journey. "Does the Wise Owl reside in this bleak setting?" she questioned. Heather had just passed by a group of dead sunflowers when a muffled voice came from nowhere.

"Please, ma'am, I lost my head. Could you give me yours?"

She turned but saw no one in sight. The voice repeated the phrase. This time, Heather gazed carefully into the decayed sunflowers and saw a man in plaid and overalls standing in the dim light with a rotted sunflower head attached to the stump of his neck. His hands were wrinkled and knotted with liver spots.

"Who are you?" Heather asked, keeping her distance.

"I lost my head, would you give me yours in exchange for this one?" the sunflower man repeated.

"No, you can't have my head," Heather returned. *Could this be the work of the scarecrow?*

"Give me your head!" the man demanded, raising his arms and reaching for her with twisted fingers. He walked toward her like a zombie. Heather screeched and scuttled down the trail while the clumsy sunflower man desperately chased after her.

"Give me your head!" he shouted again.

Her youth was no match for the decrepit being, and it disappeared into the sickly plants. Finding no trace of the partial man, she sighed in relief and sat along the side of the trail. But the withered corn behind her quivered, and out came the sunflower man again.

"Give me your head!" he ordered.

The thing reached his hand for her as she fell back in fear. The stalk he'd bent out of his way rebounded and smacked his sunflower head clean off. Hurrying down the road, Heather glanced back to see the squealing body grope the ground in search for his missing part.

She made her way down to the chimney smoke that came from behind an enclosure of wilted stalks. Heather peeped through them on her knees to see a wooden hovel with hay thatch and brick chimney in the center of the estate about twenty yards from where she was.

Hoping this was the residence of the Wise Owl, she proceeded forward until something out of the corner of her eye spooked her and made her stop in her tracks. From the left side of the front yard, she thought she had first seen cabbage sprouts in a garden, but when she looked carefully, they were not cabbages at all, but living human heads anchored into the soil. The majority of them were from the Diminished Nixis. They groaned and writhed in distress.

Sickened by this ghastly sight, Heather heard the house door open. The scarecrow walked out, holding a long-spouted flowering can. She quietly hid herself behind the diseased corn and cowered down to make sure the scarecrow couldn't see her. He made his way over to a Nixi head and shoved the tube spout into its mouth while an opalescent mixture drained into it. The head expanded about a foot in diameter to the size of a jumbo ball. When all was done, he set the can down and pulled out dentures from his pocket, placing them into his empty mouth. He then pulled a bib from his other pocket, then tied it around his neck. He picked the struggling head from the soil, where fingerlike roots dangled from its bottom, then placed it on a round platter he'd carried out with him and made his way back into the house.

"Master needs a good head," said the scarecrow in his hoarse voice that drifted from out of a broken window from the shack. Heather couldn't believe her ears when she heard a loud *crunch* from inside. It was the worst blood-curdling sound she had ever heard. Sweating from nausea, she rushed out of the blighted enclosure, ran to the left of the hidden estate, and retched.

CHAPTER

20

Daylight came to an end. The cornfield she went into, west of the scarecrow's house, was dried out, though the hardened ears were colorfully ornamental. Smog covered the cracked dirt.

Heather tried not to think about what might have happened in the cottage. The scarecrow had used the witch's magic formula to fatten the heads for eating.

"Father, is that you?" a young, innocent voice beseeched her from the ground nearby.

A neglected doll sat on a little wooden rocking chair that had chipped blue paint and a missing peg. Grime and sun had ruined his small boyish face, and the clothing had long lost its luster. The doll's blurry eyes dangled out of the sockets, so it could only see beneath him. A few black rats roamed about him but quickly scurried away when Heather approached him.

"No, I'm Heather," she softly said to him.

"Oh. My little father, the farmer's son, has not returned to get me. I need someone to take care of me."

Heather pitied the lost doll. Was there a connection between the farmer's son and the scarecrow? Another spot of sorrow emerged from the left wing of her pendant. "I will take care of you. Let me clean you up."

She dampened her handkerchief with her water and wiped his cute, tarnished face and hands. She then took a needle and thread from her shoulder sack and sewed his eyes back in.

"Thank you, Heather. Will you be my mother?"

"I certainly will," she told him sweetly. "And I shall take you home with me where you will be safe."

"Thank you," said the doll with a smile.

"Now I'll have to carry you in my shoulder sack, is that okay with you?" she asked the boy doll.

"That's fine, I can't see that well anyway," he said, and went in.

Heather continued into the dry corn patch. The black, star-studded sky had a full moon that illuminated the landscape. She at last arrived at a long, perpendicular strip of dirt that bore a dead tree with large hole in the middle of its trunk. The skull of an owl rested on the wooden floor in the center of the hole. Below the tree was a defaced tombstone and shovel, and behind the tree was a row of glowing white maize.

A card lay facedown in front of the owl's skull and she turned it over and read, "'To speak to the Wise Owl, focus the moonlight onto the skull with the lens.'"

Heather looked around the hole and found a large focusing lens with a circular frame and handle resting upright along the interior wall. She took out the lens and positioned it in between the full moon above her and the owl's skull. A bright moonbeam from way above shot into the lens onto the skeletal head, startling Heather from her stance. Nothing stirred inside the hole, but Heather caught a glimpse of an incongruous image from the mysterious lens. She situated herself carefully to focus the image without disturbing the moonbeam and saw a bluish apparition in the form of an owl standing over its skull.

"Who bears the mud pearl?" it asked.

"The Wise Owl!" Heather exclaimed. "It is I, Heather Hazelkind."

"Behind this tree is the way home. If you choose to go now, the mud pearl will vanish from your possession and be returned to the great catfish. But if you choose to save our world, you must perform a difficult task."

"What's that?" Heather asked.

"You must unearth the bones of Farmer Hagglehoff from beneath his grave near here. Wrap them with the scarecrow's skin and apply the almighty mud pearl through the eye-sockets. Once fulfilled, the great farmer will rise again and restore the land."

"How do I get the scarecrow's flesh?" she questioned.

But the owl only looked at her gravely without a word. She knew what the answer was; she had to come up with a plan herself. Finally, he asked, "Do you want to leave or save our land?"

Heather hesitated. Though she desperately wanted to go home, she realized she had vowed to restore Maizeland. If she broke that vow, she would let down the others she cared for, including Margaret Dune and the headless folk.

But her life would be at risk, and she wondered if this quest was worth dying for. After all, Heather had her whole life ahead of her. Just then, an image of Jesus Christ came to her mind. He'd sacrificed his life at a young age to salvage the good of humanity from cruel, luring sin. It was all for love. Her purpose in life was to love, despite her shortcomings and selfish desires. Love could save all at the expense of being.

Heather chose to stay.

"Brave choice," declared the owl. "Now, dig out the bones and obtain the farmer's flesh." The moonbeam vanished with the owl.

Heather put everything back the way it was found.

"It's a good thing the scarecrow's lair isn't too far from the exit," she assured herself uneasily.

Tucking away her silk coat, she took the shovel and dug her way under the tombstone with Farmer Hagglehoff's name blemished from it. Three feet underground, she hit a wooden box, and dug it out. Her shovel easily broke through the deteriorated lid where a frail sack of bones rested inside the small tomb. Heather took her time to neatly arrange the farmer's skeleton on the ground and then walked back into the piebald cornfield to face the scarecrow once more.

CHAPTER

21

She hesitated to move toward that house. It was either subdue the scarecrow or possibly get killed by him. A few times she turned back to the tree of the Wise Owl but then resumed her course.

As she struggled to come up with a plan to get the scarecrow's flesh, the shape of Mr. Cob's face materialized from an ear in front of her.

"You're very brave, Heather. I'm proud of you," he told her with a face richly decorated in orange, red, and purple.

"Mr. Cob! You look dashing!" she said.

"You have made it this far, but now is the time for your greatest challenge yet. If you can immobilize the scarecrow, you can remove his stuffing."

"I can't see how that is physically possible. He's inhumanly strong and violently psychotic," she argued.

"Be very cautious and clever, Heather. Remember, the golden spirit is with you. Good luck."

He left her on the most dangerous mission yet. She thought if she could take away his sickle, it would be easier to unstuff him.

Taking slow, quiet steps toward the demented house, the Indian corn from her side ruffled.

"I want your head!" snarled the scarecrow, and swiped at her. His sickle snagged her skirt as she fled in terror.

"I want your *head*!" he bellowed in wrath, swatting everywhere.

Heather randomly switched directions in the field to lose him. All the multicolored ears around the beast projected out from their husks and into the air like guided missiles. They darted to the ground like knives, yet Heather managed to not get hit by sheer luck, save for the tear in her skirt. That was the first time she had witnessed his sorcery, and it chilled her blood to think of what else he was capable of doing.

Heather and the scarecrow wandered aimlessly in the corn without knowing each other's whereabouts. She then entered a circular gap in the dry maizefield, unexpectedly finding the fat pig she met on the way to the witch's hut, lazing around in the center of the open area.

"Hello, little Madam," the pig said with a smile. "I just stopped to rest a bit, since my belly is almost full."

"Oh, please, Mr. Pig! You must flee from here, for there is a mad scarecrow on his way!" she said desperately.

"What kind of leaves is he made of?" the pig asked her.

She paused to wonder why he had asked her that.

"Heather!" another voice shouted. The Armadillo Knight came dashing into the open space from the cornstalks to her right. "I just came from a hard-fought battle. I heard screaming. Are you all right?"

Heather glanced back and forth at the pig and the armadillo until a spark entered her mind. "I have an idea!" she told them.

After huddling with her companions, she headed back out to find the scarecrow.

"Mr. Scarecrow!" she called with false confidence. "I'm here, you walking bag of flesh! Come and behead me!"

The maize shuffled from her side and the scarecrow swung his sharp sickle down to her, slashing her shoulder as she darted in retreat. She sprinted desperately toward the circular yawn, but before she reached it, a couple of enchanted stalks wrapped around her. She squawked, trying to wiggle loose, but to no avail. Now she was definitely bound to lose her head and end up in the cabbage patch with the others.

Heather, shuddering in fear, thought hard with precious little time as the monster from hell approached her with lifeless eyes.

What do I do? she thought to herself. The heat from her face generated by anxiety caused her forehead to sweat. *All right, this land is magical, so I must use magic to help me. What have I learned? What will work that makes sense?*

The scarecrow was getting closer.

What can make me go up? Not the dust bowl; I have no control over that. The words "stuck" and "up" resonated repeatedly in her mind. Then an epiphany struck.

Dance like a mudskipper! she remembered at last.

Heather tap-danced the quick movement the mudskippers had taught her and the cracked dirt lifted beneath her. The roots loosened, and she dashed back to her recent rendezvous before the beast could claim her life. Heather hid, leaving the pig to face the scarecrow as they'd planned.

"Hmm…you look as though you're full of hot tamales," the pig said to the foe upon his entrance.

"I need heads!" declared the scarecrow, and he swatted at the pig's neck.

The pig's hide, however, was too thick for the sickle to have any piercing effect, and it bounced off the pig's neck, like striking rubber. "Heh, heh. That tickles," giggled the pig. "Now, can I chomp on your stuffing, Mr. Scarecrow?"

The Armadillo Knight somersaulted into view and knocked over the scarecrow in front of the fat pig.

The sickle flew from his hand. The swine violently thrashed and chomped through the scarecrow's skin to access the leaf shavings, like a bear mauling a grown man.

Heather moved in afterward to obtain the farmer's flesh.

"That hit the spot!" declared the satiated pig.

"Oh, thank you Mr. Pig!" she said with glee, hugging him tenderly and scratching his back thoroughly. "Forgive me if I ever doubted you for one moment."

"My pleasure, little madam," the pig returned.

"Oh, thank you Armadillo Knight!" she praised the warrior with a warm hug. "You helped me disarm the scarecrow. I couldn't have done it without you."

"It is my honor, Ms. Hazelkind. My work here is finished now that the scarecrow's terror is no more."

"I shall take this skin and restore the land!" exclaimed Heather.

"What are you waiting for?" said the armadillo excitedly.

She pranced to the grave of bones in triumph.

After healing her wound with the magic silk, she slowly approached the skeleton and fanned the skin out to carefully cover the bones with it. Suddenly, the essence of the scarecrow awakened, and the skin forced itself on Heather, choking her with its arms. She struggled to breathe and tried to free her neck, but the force was too great. The flat face of the scarecrow snarled at her, "I want your head!" She fell to the ground and the bulk of the possessed skin wrapped around her neck and squeezed like a boa constrictor.

Heather tried with all her might to remove the flesh from her, but he was too strong. She continued to gasp for air and then felt lightheaded. Her ears rang.

Time slowed to a crawl.

Heather closed her eyes, ready to die, but then she felt Margaret Dune's loving presence. A light source emanated through her eyelids and she opened them to find her ladybug pendant glowing bright red. She grabbed the pendant and touched the scarecrow's flesh with it. The skin weakened from the touch of love and she took in one large, relieved breath of air.

Heather could unwrap the skin from her neck, though the scarecrow still resisted with reduced strength. He gnarred at her. Then she hunched forward and used her weight to lay him flat onto the bones. She reached for her shoulder sack with her free hand to get the mud pearl, but the scarecrow's flat arm moved in to restrain her hand.

"You die!" he rasped.

She could feel his strength return. Heather grabbed her purse strap with her teeth and swung the bag toward her free hand by jerking her head. Once it was within reach, she unzipped the bag and reached in to retrieve the pearl. She held it tightly and tried to reach for his eye socket, but his grip on her hand was too tight.

Heather then scowled at him and said, "No. You die!" She took the pearl into her mouth, leaned over to his head like she was going to kiss him and spat the pearl into his eye socket.

The body rejuvenated its rotted flesh, gaining a healthy skin tone and texture. New blood vessels branched out as muscles rematerialized. Eyeballs developed and, finally, a complete human being was reborn.

The handsome farmer awoke, mystified, asking, "Where am I? What happened?"

"You're safe, Farmer Hagglehoff," she said to him kindly. "You're human again. Now you must restore the land."

"What land?" asked the farmer, all bewildered.

"Maizeland," replied Heather.

"Maizeland!" The farmer stood up and scanned the ruined terrain. "Oh no!"

Farmer Hagglehoff faced the sky with open arms and declared, "My good land, let there be peace again!"

Blue shooting stars glided throughout the sky, like the Fourth of July. The maize all around suddenly shined beautifully like gold perched on emeralds, some of which *were* gold. The soil glittered with sparkly streamlets. It was wonderful.

"Hello, Heather," a voice behind her called.

She turned toward the tree and saw four people walking toward her. She couldn't recognize their faces but then recognized their clothing. It was the Headless Folk with their original heads.

"Sally, Bobby, Percy, Lilly! You're all normal!" she exclaimed happily.

"You've freed us, my dear. We knew you could do it all along," said Sally.

"I'm very happy for you all," Heather said.

"Hello, Heather. Recognize me?" A partially bald man wearing a Western duster coat greeted her whose voice and grin seemed strangely familiar to her. Then she realized who he was.

"Mr. Cob!" she said.

"You've helped me remember my name. It's Henry Jo. And I can now remember my full life," he said, but then frowned. "Unfortunately, my family was taken away by a tornado."

"Oh, I'm so sorry, Henry," she said.

"But now that you've freed me, I no longer have a need to return to your world. I can stay here and help Farmer Hagglehoff lead the land."

"You have my sincere support, sir," Heather said. "You gave me plenty of comfort on my journey."

"It was bizarre how I became a cob," he said. "When I was transported to this world, I came across an unusual cornstalk whose ear reflected my image. I got this strange sense that it could read my mind before it even spoke, and then it asked me what I really wanted in life. It communicated not through voice but through thought, and it felt cold and callous. I could have dismissed it, but I was emotionally weak after I lost my family to a tornado the previous year. I responded in my mind that I would rather disappear and be forgotten. It was then that I found myself trapped in that ear for a seeming eternity with no one to notice me. At first, I didn't mind it since I was so depressed, but then I quickly panicked and wanted out of this imprisonment. The strange voice laughed and then granted me limited domain within the cornstalks, limited memory of my former self, and limited communication with other beings."

"I am so glad you are free with friends around you now," Heather said.

"Thank you. Perhaps it was best that I didn't remember who I was, but that isn't a good thing to have. We must reconcile with our fears, guilts, and remorse to overcome emotional pain in our lives."

"Well said, Henry. We are all here for you," Sally Breen told him. She then turned her attention to

Heather and said, "Heather, I think someone special is coming to meet you." Sally pointed to a person walking up to her from the beautiful cornstalks.

A handsome lad around her age came into focus with a warm smile. His face had red freckles on the nose and cheeks. His hair was golden-brown and his right eye was blue and his left eye was brown.

Her heart filled with nostalgia and her eyes watered before she managed to say, "Lempet?"

He nodded. She opened her arms out and they embraced warmly. Her love for him couldn't be worded, and they leaned heads together.

"I'm so glad you didn't die in vain after all," she said to him. "I didn't know you were once human."

"Yes. I was abandoned here as a baby, but Crempet named me and raised me in the water. After spending most of my life there, I became a fish. From there on, I served the mud pearl till my death. Now that the wicked curse of the scarecrow is lifted, I am free to go as a human again."

"I really appreciated your company. You will always have a place in my heart," she lovingly told him. Heather was so overjoyed that her throat tightened, ready to cry. The sixth spot of joy on the right wing of Heather's ladybug pendant was revealed.

Farmer Hagglehoff then smiled at her as she approached him at last.

"Farmer Hagglehoff, you are my hero. It must have been very painful being a scarecrow."

"Indeed so. But, you're the true heroine, my dear," he said. "We only helped you a little in getting here."

"I couldn't have done it without you all," she said.

"Very true. But we were waiting for a long time to find someone pure of heart that could bare the mud pearl. Years ago, I established the farm you saw in the real world only as an extension of a beautiful, wild maize field I came upon. After working hard, I got transported to this realm that is really a fairy land made by the Goddess of Gold, an angel of high order, whose spirit still resides within the corn. Native Americans were known to venture through here as a land of hope. Upon hearing that I was the owner of the farm back home, the Fairy Goddess appointed me as king of the land before leaving with all her fairies. I was to maintain the peace for all of Maizeland and to feed the earth. I made a lot of money back home and, in fact, became so in love with my business that I nearly forgot about my own family."

The farmer paused, flattened his face, then continued in a solemn tone.

"I'll fill you in on a little secret, Heather. This may sound disturbing to you. When I was six years old, I lived in Ukraine when it was part of the Soviet Union. The country was called the 'Breadbasket of Europe' since we grew very rich in wheat. However, an evil famine of unparalleled proportions was imposed. I was the only one left in my family to survive and escape to a great and loving nation, America."

"How tragic!" exclaimed Sally Breen.

"A German-American family living in the Midwest adopted me and taught me everything there was to know about farming. As I grew up and had a family of my own, I never wanted anyone to go hungry in their homeland again. I was blessed to find this magical land and harvested it as much as I could to feed the world. I was so determined after what had happened to me that I actually became obsessed. As I said, I neglected my own family, as if I had totally forgotten them, the most important thing to me. One day, the business was getting a little rough, and my six-year-old boy got in trouble at school. After feeling frustrated with myself, I regretfully struck him, and he ran off into the fields never to come back. After days of him missing, I panicked and searched up and down the fields day and night in both worlds with my sickle. One morning, I came across my son's doll lying in the stalks close at home and knew he must have been close. As I searched further, I at last found him. To my horror, he was run over by a tractor in a terrible accident. Nobody really knows how it happened."

"Oh, my gosh! That's awful!" said Heather in deep sorrow. The seventh spot of sorrow emerged from the left wing of her ladybug pendant due to the farmer's tragic life.

"It was so awful my wife left me, and I had no one but myself," continued the saddened farmer. "No parent should ever have to bury their children. I blamed myself for this catastrophe and started hating my life, as it saw one tragedy after the other. While wandering into the fields reaping endlessly, an evil presence whispered into my ear one day. I didn't know what or where it came from, but I knew it wasn't pleasant as I felt untold terror from its voice that could only be heard through my mind. I didn't trust it at first, but then it tried to convince me that my whole life was a lie—that nothing mattered and that being a good and loving human being was pointless, if not an outright burden. That the tragedies I experienced were evident, and trying to be good and just brings more pain and disappointment. It convinced me to give up pursuing the 'falsehood' of love and undo it. Hence, I became a mindless scarecrow destined to destroy what is good. Without a loving soul left in me, the mystical land suffered. To save the business, my step-nephews luckily took over before foreclosure. Meanwhile, I became more and more mad, and needed a saving grace. You, Heather, were my virtuous counterpart that I was missing for so long. The purity and wisdom of the pearl was in you the whole time, and it wouldn't have worked otherwise."

"It seems that sometimes in life we get real big and forget who we once were," said Sally Breen. "It is the small things, the little happy things that matter to us in the end."

"Very true, Mrs. Breen," said Farmer Hagglehoff. "The fairies enchanted the mud pearl in order to counter the forces of evil. When learning about the troubles of Maizeland, Crempet, the Fairy Goddess' favorite minion, took the vulnerable pearl into his magic belly and waited for a special person to come restore me. Your brave and unselfish choices, even in the face of danger, helped many in need, Heather—something I was unable to do. Now this land is once again peaceful and beautiful so anyone may enjoy its riches. Thank you."

Heather smiled.

"I see an interesting parallel between your downfall and mine, Bill," said Henry Jo to the farmer. "We were both seduced by an evil presence at our lowest point in life. What could it be? Where did it come from?"

"I wish I knew, Henry," answered Farmer Hagglehoff. "It definitely had no connection with the Goddess of Gold. It was her opposite, and it was preying on our woes and vulnerabilities. That's why we must reject evil in all its forms."

"Yes!" said Heather. "Mr. Hagglehoff, do you remember sending me a message asking for help on one of those special cornstalks while you were still a scarecrow?"

"No! I don't remember that," he answered.

"You did. And that was evident that your loving soul was still living inside the scarecrow."

"Wow!" he exclaimed.

"I think I have something you may want to keep." Heather took out the doll she found early on and showed it to him.

He brightened. "My son's doll!"

She handed the doll over to him. "This will be your new father," she told the little boy.

"Hello," he greeted the farmer tenderly. Farmer Hagglehoff's eyes filled with tears.

"What was your boy's name?" Heather asked the farmer.

"Fin," he replied.

"Maybe you should name your son's doll 'Fin'," she suggested.

"What a good idea," he agreed. "I will fix him up and cherish him with all my love."

"I hope the fairies return some day," said Sally.

"They will," replied the farmer.

"The Goddess of Gold probably sent you here, Heather," Sally told her.

"Yes," Heather replied.

"What did you learn, Ms. Hazelkind?" asked Henry Jo.

"Lots," she said. "One thing I did learn about the most is love. One can be the most powerful person in the world yet still be lost. We all must learn to love and keep loving no matter how hard or tragic life can be, for all that really matters in the end is one another."

"Wonderful," said Henry.

"Now, do you wish to stay or return home?" asked the farmer.

She closed her eyes, breathed in the fresh air, and smiled brightly. Heather acknowledged the marvelous peace all around her as she had grown to love it over the course of her journey, but she knew she had to go back.

"I love this land very much, but I wish to return and share my light with those I love, including my students and family back home. My golden spirit is calling to me," she said.

"We support you all the way, Ms. Hazelkind," said Farmer Hagglehoff. "From now on, if you wish to return to Maizeland, just enter any cornfield with your silk coat, and it will bring you here."

"Thank you. And God bless you all," she said to them with happy tears.

"Goodbye, Heather," the Armadillo Knight and fat pig called to her. "We will miss you."

"Bye-bye. And God bless you, too," she replied joyfully. "I'll miss you all." The party stood around her as she exited the last row of cornstalks. A bright light surrounded her. She looked back at her waving friends and noticed they were frozen in time. A strange tunnel of energy propelled her forward and she could hear the vibration of the vortex. It sounded like beautiful bells, hums, and horns. A sequence of images revealing her whole journey flashed before her eyes and then flashed in reverse order upon hearing the phrase "One can change many" echo in her mind. Then everything went dark.

CHAPTER

22

Heather opened her eyes and found herself lying in an ordinary cornfield next to a dirt road in broad daylight. She slowly stood up and heard Farmer Patterson's voice holler to her.

"Ms. Hazelkind!"

Heather looked about the dirt road and saw him hustling over to her, panting.

"Ms. Hazelkind!" he called again before meeting up with her. "Thank goodness we found you! You were gone for about an hour."

"Just an hour?" she exclaimed, befuddled.

"Are you okay?" he asked her.

"I'm fine," she assured him.

"I'm sorry about the wagon. I just ordered it to be fixed right away. It will never happen again. Looks like you had some adventure, huh?"

"Yes, as a matter of fact, I did have quite an adventure," she replied with an ill-suppressed laugh.

"I'll get the children," he said in happy relief, and ran off to get them.

Heather confirmed that she was still wearing her ladybug pendant, and then opened her shoulder sack to see if the silk coat was there, proving her journey had happened. It was in there, shining as gorgeously as ever. She looked back at the cornfield where the honeybees were out gathering pollen from the tassels.

"The bees returned!" she exclaimed to herself, thinking Queen Nonabi and Margaret Dune must have been very happy. The pleasure of being back home caused the appearance of the last spot of joy on the right wing of Heather's ladybug pendant.

Having completed seven joys and seven sorrows on her journey, she held up her necklace in remembrance of Margaret. Just then, she caught sight of Mrs. Dune facing her within a row of cornstalks in the background. Heather heard her whisper, "Thank you, Heather."

The ladybug pendant glowed ruby red in Heather's hand. She released it from her fingers and it came to life as a real ladybug. It flew off into the horizon. Heather raised her head to the clouds and smiled brightly, then looked back to see Margaret, but she was gone.

All her little students ran to her and gave her warm hugs. It was such a joyful reunion that she tried hiding away more tears.

"Where were you?" they asked her.

"Out there." She pointed to the giant cornfield.

"Will we be back?" a little one asked.

Heather smiled and then said, "There will always be a special place for us even when it's not in our sight."

Her students walked with her back to the school bus.

The End

ACKNOWLEDGEMENTS

I would like to sincerely thank all the people I'm about to mention for their hard work, expertise, and dedication in helping me deliver magic to my first novel, *Into the Magic Cornfield*. Their efforts could not be appreciated more.

First, I would like to greatly thank my top-rated illustrator from Fiverr, Doan Trang, whose incredible artistic talent strengthened the vitality of the world I built. Her serious and passionate devotion to the fine arts, especially in children's literature, cannot be understated.

I would also like to thank my editor, GrammarMaven of ServiceScape, for her literary expertise in creative writing that includes many genres. Her keen eye for character and story development as well as spelling and grammar made me into a better writer. The advice and suggestions she offered were invaluable.

I would like to thank my beta reader, Amber Winter from Fiverr, for her kind and constructive honesty in assessing my book before publication. Her tactful comments and opinions about each chapter were valuable to me as a conscientious writer.

I thank my book designer for beautifying the layout of my novel for printing, and my parents and grandparent for their support and encouragement.

Lastly, I would like to thank my friend Jean Paulsen who was my first unofficial test reader of my unedited manuscript. Her practical critiquing was crucial in me reworking material that was incongruous to the genre.

Writing a book is hard work, and it really takes a good team to get it done right. I thank this team tremendously.

Todd Bernacil was born in Livermore, California. He graduated from California Polytechnic State University with a bachelor's degree in Biological Sciences, and later received a master's degree in Forensic DNA and Serology at the University of Florida. He currently works in the chemical industry and dabbles in computer programming and creative writing as hobbies. He grew up intrigued by European and American fairy tales, including the works of the Brothers Grimm, *Alice in Wonderland*, and the *Wizard of Oz*. He likes working out at the gym, going for nature walks, playing the piano, and spending time in Sonora, Gold Rush Country, with friends and family.

ABOUT THE ILLUSTRATOR

Doan Trang is a skilled artist who specializes in line art, illustration, and concept art. Children's book illustrations are her favorite endeavors. She lives in Vietnam and works as a freelancer. She studied Animation at Nanyang Technological University and has always had a strong passion for the fine arts. She enjoys picking up new hobbies and playing with her three dogs.

Made in the USA
San Bernardino, CA
27 April 2019